L. D. KNORR

The

Rest Area Murder

The RV Mysteries
Book TWO

The Rest Area Murder

FIRST SUNBURY PRESS EDITION
Printed in the United States of America
July 2012

Trade Paperback ISBN: 978-1-62006-083-4
Mobipocket format (Kindle) ISBN: 978-1-62006-084-1
ePub format (Nook) ISBN: 978-1-62006-085-8

Published by:
Sunbury Press
Camp Hill, PA
www.sunburypress.com

Camp Hill, Pennsylvania   USA

Acknowledgments

Thank you to my editor Jennifer Melendrez who corrected the thousand and one punctuation errors and whose suggestions made it a far better book.

Thanks to my wife Emily for making vital suggestions for the book and for tolerating my full-time retired presence while I commandeered a corner of our living room for my portable writing desk.

Thank you Sunbury Press for publishing my work.

And last but not least, a salute to all the millions of RVers across the country seeking adventure. I wish you smooth highways and level campsites.

Chapter - 1

Hank and Helen Moran were back in Kenner, Louisiana, planning their belated motorhome tour. The tour had been temporarily put on hold when they were sidelined by their investigation of a series of murders during their shakedown cruise to Biloxi, Mississippi.

Hank had only retired three weeks prior from the Kenner, Louisiana Police Department, where he was a homicide detective for the past thirty two years. The sixty year old detective and his wife purchased a Fleetwood Bounder motorhome and planned to do extensive summer traveling. Since Hank and Helen wouldn't immediately be needed as witnesses for the trial of Franklin Whitehead, they were ready and anxious to once again hit the road.

"Well, Helen, it looks like our tour will take about two months. We'll wend our way north to the U.P. of Michigan, travel across Canada to Montreal, then pick our way back down to Louisiana with stops at whatever interesting places we see along the way."

Helen said, "Don't forget that I want to spend a few days in Lancaster County, Pennsylvania to see Amish country. You know I'm a big fan of the Heritage Series of books. I want to see firsthand where the stories took place."

Besides the several stops they had mutually agreed upon, Helen and Hank negotiated stops along the way that pertained to their individual tastes as well. Hank said he would stop at the various mansions that Helen enjoyed touring if she agreed to visit places like the Grand Ole Opry. Hank was a big fan of Bluegrass Music and they both enjoyed sites historical in nature.

Helen said, "Hank, don't forget that we promised the Anspachs we would stop in for a visit on our way north."

"They're on the list," Hank replied. "We should be at their place in less than two weeks."

They had met the Anspachs on their maiden voyage to Biloxi. Bill Anspach was a retired editor for the *Indianapolis Star*, and still wrote a weekly travel column when on the road with his wife in their Winnebago. Bill wrote about interesting places they visited and people they met. He wrote a series of articles about the revival preacher and the Leviticus murders in which Hank and Helen played a major part in solving the crimes.

With the motorhome packed for an extended journey they turned off the water to their house, set the burglar alarm, locked up, and were on their way. Their "toad"—the vehicle they towed behind their motorhome for use as a runabout once the RV was hooked up to the utilities at a site—was Helen's Honda Civic.

Both Hank and Helen were huge Elvis fans, so the first stop on their tour was Tupelo, Mississippi, to see the King's birthplace. Helen, who was reading from a travel brochure she picked up at the last rest area on Interstate 55, said,"Hank, listen to this! "She quoted from the brochure, "It was once said Elvis's boyhood home, a two room shotgun house, could fit into one room of the Graceland mansion. Wow! Talk about a close-knit family." She went on reading, "The house was built in 1934 by Elvis's father, Vernon, with help from his Uncle Vester and grandfather, Jesse."

"That was right in the middle of the Depression. I wonder how they paid for the materials." Hank said.

"You can ask that question when we get there, dear."

A short time later they pulled into the parking lot of Elvis's boyhood home and museum. Hank was pleased that there was parking for motor coaches, as they had time to tour the house and museum before checking into the campground at Barnes Crossing.

While touring the house, Hank learned that Vernon Presley borrowed one hundred and eighty dollars to build the house from the man who owned the dairy farm he worked on. Elvis was born in the house the next year. A few years later, the house was lost when Vernon Presley was convicted for check forgery and sentenced to three years in the Mississippi State Penitentiary at Parchman.

After checking into the campground at Barnes Crossing, Helen prepared a light shrimp scampi microwave dinner for two. With the minimal cleanup required, they had time to take the Early Years Driving Tour, which included the school the young Elvis attended and the hardware store where he bought his first guitar. The Morans were amazed at Elvis's humble beginnings, and their excitement built in anticipation of their next stop at Graceland.

The next morning they were excited to be on their way to the second stop on their itinerary, Memphis, Tennessee, and Elvis's Graceland mansion. Three hours later they arrived at the Graceland RV Park and Campground, located right behind the Heartbreak Hotel. The RV park was within walking distance of Graceland directly across Elvis Presley Boulevard.

The next morning they were up bright and early and made the nine a.m. tour. Helen was near the back of the tour group in the Graceland living room when she felt a sudden cool movement of air on the back of her neck. When she turned around she caught a glimpse of a dark haired man in a white jumpsuit passing by the room opening. When she looked down the hall no one was there, but she caught a fleeting glimpse of someone dressed in white turning away at the top of the stairs. Helen told the tour guide, "I think it's cool you have someone dressed as Elvis for the tour."

The tour guide looked a little puzzled and said, "Excuse me, ma'am?"

Helen repeated, "I think it's cool that you have an Elvis impersonator following the group."

The tour guide said, "Ma'am we have no one dressed as Elvis for the tour."

Helen insisted, "But I just saw him walk by the entrance to the room."

Hank knew better than to say something that would embarrass Helen in front of the group, so he just kept quiet.

The tour guide, taking advantage of the incident, said, "Other people have seen Elvis. Sometimes hurrying up the stairs and occasionally in the Jungle Room. People have also claimed they saw him sitting in front of a window when they looked back at the building."

Helen said, "Holy cow! And I thought it was an impersonator."

Hank offered, "Apparently Elvis never left the building."

Hank's much overused remark produced only a few muted chuckles from the group.

As the tour guide led the group to the dining room she apologized for the mess in the hall, as some second floor rooms were being repainted. The second floor, she informed them,was a private residence and was not open to the public tour.

As Hank passed by the hall he noticed a dark haired painter in a white painter's jumpsuit, busy with a paint roller at the top of the stairs. He grinned widely and thought it best not to mention it to Helen that Elvis was now doing renovation work in the mansion. He thought, *Perhaps Elvis stepped outside for a smoke break and rushed by the living room when he went back to work.* Hank couldn't stifle his grin the whole remainder of the tour.

At the end of the tour Helen had to make a stop in the Graceland gift shop. She couldn't leave Graceland without a memento of their visit. In the corner of a display case she spied a gold plated "Taking Care of Business" bracelet she just had to have. It was reasonably priced in Hank's estimation so he presented his credit card to the clerk. He found a Graceland shot glass to add to his collection, which he had started on their recent trip to Biloxi. Then he spied a book called the "Elvis Handbook." Paging through it he saw that it was a comprehensive history of Elvis, from birth to death, with many fascinating photos. The book was quickly added to the bill, as he was sure it would provide interesting reading on quiet nights at the campgrounds.

The next day was spent on the tour of Sun Studios and a trek on Beale Street; Elvis, Jerry Lee Lewis, and Johnny Cash made their first hit recordings at Sun. The original soundstage and microphone where Elvis recorded "That's All Right" was still on display. It gave Helen goosebumps to imagine all her favorite stars gracing the small facility.

Their stroll up and down Beale Street was punctuated by the blues emanating from the open doorways of the many clubs, including B.B. King's. After a dinner of barbecued ribs and a session of sittin, listenin, and sippin, the Morans retreated to the serene atmosphere of their motorhome.

They were leaving for Nashville in the morning and both agreed that Memphis was definitely on their list of places to return to for a longer stay.

The leg of their journey from Memphis to Nashville was a straight shot on Interstate 40, and four and one half hours later they pulled into the Two Rivers Campground two miles north of Opryland.

The first order of business was a late afternoon tour of the Ryman Auditorium in downtown Nashville. The Morans had their picture taken on center stage as a keepsake. The tour guide gave a brief but interesting history of the building. He explained to them, "The Ryman was the home of the Grand Ole Opry broadcasts from 1943 to 1974. It was originally built in 1892 as the Union Gospel Tabernacle by a boisterous riverboat captain and saloon owner named Thomas Ryman. Originally a house of worship, the Ryman earned the nickname the 'Mother Church of Country Music.' Performances are still held at the Ryman but the main venue is now the Grand Ole Opry House on Opryland Drive."

Hank and Helen took in a Vince Gill and Amy Grant show at the Grand Ole Opry the next evening. The morning of the show was spent on a tour of the Belmont Mansion.

Helen read aloud from the brochure, "The Belmont Mansion played a role in the Civil War Battle of Nashville as one of the Union command centers. The battle was fought on December 15th and 16th, 1864. The Confederate Army of Tennessee under Lt. Gen. John Bell Hood was largely destroyed as a fighting force by the Union forces under Maj. Gen. George H. Thomas."

Helen also read, "The Belmont Mansion is the largest house museum in Tennessee. The home's history revolved around a woman by the name of Adelicia Hayes Franklin

Acklen Cheatham." Helen paused a moment then said, "I think I'm going to add a few other names between 'Helen' and 'Moran.' My name is too simple."

Hank informed Helen, "Do you realize that at least two of Adelicia's middle names are the surnames of deceased husbands? Isn't it best that you keep your name simple?"

Helen replied, "Hmm, I guess I'll keep my name simple as long as you don't take it upon yourself to defuse any more bombs like you did a few weeks ago."

Hank retorted, "I'll promise not to defuse any more bombs if you promise not to hide under any more strange beds."

"Touché. You have yourself a deal, big boy."

After an additional day spent in Nashville, mostly relaxing at the campgrounds pool, they were once again on the road. The next two days included a stop at Abraham Lincoln's birthplace near Hodgenville, Kentucky, and a stay-over in Louisville to tour the Louisville Slugger Factory and Museum.

The next leg of their journey was the short hundred miles to Indianapolis to pay the promised visit to the Anspachs.

Midway to Indy, they stopped at the I-65 rest area two miles north of Columbus. Hank wanted to add an Indiana map to his collection of state maps. Helen was pleased that she could use the motorhome's facilities rather than the public rest rooms.

Hank was walking to the public facilities from the rest area's truck and RV parking lot when he heard two sharp gunshot reports, loud mufflers, and a squeal of rubber on asphalt. He turned and saw a dark green pickup truck rapidly bearing down on him. He barely managed to hot step it out of the way as the truck sped by. Two men were in the truck: one young driver and an older passenger. The young driver had a large red birthmark on the left side of his face. In his distressed state he failed to note the truck's tag number, but did see it was from Michigan. Hank's eyes were drawn to the truck's back window where he saw an iron cross decal on the driver's side and a dual lightning bolt decal on the passenger side. As the truck sped away, he was beside himself that he didn't get the tag number. It was the one piece of information an experienced homicide detective should have garnered.

Hank heard a woman's wail and turned and saw a Hispanic woman on her knees, sobbing over a body laying face up on the ground. She kept screaming the name "Agusto."

Hank strode quickly to the scene. There was a man of Hispanic descent lying in a rapidly growing pool of blood. One bullet hole was visible in the center of his chest and one in the left shoulder. Hank yelled for someone to call 911 and to tell them an ambulance was needed. A lady with a cell phone to her ear said she was already talking with the 911 dispatcher.

Hank knelt and pressed his fingers to the man's carotid artery but felt no pulse. He looked across the body at the still kneeling woman and shook his head.

Just then Helen appeared behind Hank and saw the woman begin to swoon. Hank and Helen both caught her before she collapsed. When she appeared to recover, Helen asked the woman her name. She said, "My name is Maria Soto and that is my husband, Agusto, on the ground. And this is our son Eduardo." Eduardo had just arrived on the scene after using the facilities.

Helen and Eduardo helped Maria to her feet and walked with her a short distance to a bench positioned along the footwalk. Eduardo, who appeared to be about twelve years old, sat beside his mother in an apparent state of bewilderment.

The Indiana State Police cruiser and the ambulance arrived in tandem. By now a crowd of onlookers had assembled, many of whom had never seen a dead body as the result of a cold-blooded murder. Hank, exuding an air of authority, kept everyone back at a respectable distance. Helen sat with the Sotos on the bench and tried to console Maria.

Maria said, sobbing, "I don't know what we are going to do. Agusto is the only one who could drive. We are from

Little Rock and we were traveling to visit my brother, Felix, who lives near Indianapolis. We were almost there."

Helen said, "Maria, my husband and I are on our way to Indianapolis also. I can drive your car the rest of the way if you want to continue to your brother's house. At a time like this you need to be with someone close. Once you and Eduardo are with your relatives you can better make decisions about your immediate future."

Maria answered, "Thank you for your offer, but I must call my brother first. Perhaps he can come and get us."

Helen looked up to see that a state police officer had appeared and likely wanted to question the Sotos.

"Ma'am, I am Officer Bricker. I am so sorry for your loss. Are you able to talk and tell me what happened?"

Maria stated, "Yes, I was beside my husband when he was shot. A truck stopped beside us with two men in it. The driver called us 'fuckin wetbacks.' Then he fired through the open window of the truck and sped off. We are not illegal. We are US citizens. My husband, Agusto, is an engineer. He got his degree from the University of Arkansas."

Officer Bricker asked, "Can you describe the man who did the shooting?"

"Yes, I can. He was young with brown hair. He had a big red birthmark on the side of his face. I could definitely identify him if I saw him again."

Bricker continued, "Can you describe the man in the passenger seat?"

"No, I didn't get a good look at him. All I remember is that he looked older."

"What about your son? Did he see anything?

"No, Eduardo was still in the rest room when it happened."

There were at least seven other witnesses to the shooting, and all said that the shooter drove a green pickup truck, either a Chevrolet or GMC. They all had varying descriptions of the occupants.

When questioned, Hank was the only witness who recalled the Michigan license tag. He told Officer Bricker that the back window caught his attention and it was the reason he failed to record the tag number. He described the iron cross and lightning bolt decals, noting that both decals were known symbols of the white supremacy movement. Officer Bricker handed Hank his card in the hopes he would recall the tag number and call him.

Agusto Soto was pronounced dead at the scene and was taken to the Bartholomew County Coroner's Office four miles south in Columbus.

In talking to her brother on the cell phone, Maria learned that Felix had just broken his ankle and could not drive. He had been trying to use his son's skateboard and took a tumble.

After disconnecting from Felix, Maria said to Helen, "I am sorry to have to ask you, but I need to accept your offer to drive us the rest of the way to Indianapolis. I know the way to my brother's house and could direct you."

Helen replied, "It's no problem, Maria. I'll be glad to help you."

As a backup, Hank programmed the address into the motorhome's GPS system. Helen drove the Sotos' late model Durango the forty five miles to Indianapolis while Hank followed in the motorhome.

Felix, on crutches, and his wife, Anita, were waiting on their front porch when the entourage pulled up in front of their modest ranch house. Felix greeted the Morans with a handshake and said, "I don't know how I can thank you enough for being so kind to Maria. Please come in."

"We would like to accept your invitation, but we must be on our way," Helen said. "Now is the time for your family to grieve privately without strangers in your house."

Maria gave Helen a long hug and said, "Thank you again, Mrs. Moran, for driving Eduardo and me here."

Helen replied, "It was the least I could do, Maria. I am so sorry for your loss and I just can't imagine what you must be going through."

The Morans left and drove the additional five miles to the Lake Haven Retreat campground. Hank called Bill Anspach to tell him they had arrived in Indy.

Bill answered, recognizing Hank's number, "Hello, Hank. Are you in the neighborhood?

"Yes, we are, Bill, but I think it's a tad late to make a visit this evening. We had a delay on the way up here"

"How about if you come tomorrow afternoon, Hank? Jenny and I will go pick up a few choice steaks and we'll have a backyard barbecue."

"Can't turn that down, Bill. We'll see you and Jenny tomorrow then."

Helen had a restless night's sleep thinking about Maria Soto and how she was coping with her loss. To be traveling on what was planned to be a joyous vacation and lose a husband and the father of their only child was a tragedy that should not have happened. Helen prayed that the person responsible for the unthinkable crime would be brought to justice.

The next afternoon, Bill Anspach was preparing the barbecue when the Morans arrived. Bill and Hank shook hands, and Bill greeted Helen with a hug. Bill's wife, Jenny, came bounding out the house and gave both Helen and Hank hugs. Helen then followed Jenny back into the house, and Bill told Hank to grab a beer from the cooler while the charcoal heated up.

Bill said, "I had one of those gas grills once, but you just can't beat the flavor left by real charcoal."

Hank replied, "I fully agree with you, but with always being on call at my old job, I had to settle for the speed of my gas grill."

"Hank, I told you last month you need to relax and start enjoying life now that you're retired. Stop and smell the roses, and enjoy the aroma of cooking on real charcoal. And besides, this is why beer was invented."

"I don't understand, Bill. Why was beer invented?"

"Hell, Hank, it makes the wait for the charcoal to heat up bearable. Oh, by the way, I saw on the news yesterday where a guy was murdered at the I-65 rest area just south of here. You didn't happen to run into it on your way north, did you?"

"You're not going to believe this, but then again you might. I was nearly run down by the shooter when he was making his getaway."

"Hank, it's beginning to sound like you're not meant to enjoy yourself. How do you keep getting yourself into the middle of these things?"

"I don't know, Bill, I guess I'm just lucky."

Hank proceeded to tell Bill the story of the rest area murder and how Helen volunteered to drive the Sotos' car the rest of the way to Indy. He explained that the state police investigation and all was the reason they arrived so late in Indy.

Jenny came out of the house carrying a plate full of steaks for grilling and Helen was right behind her with a tray full of potatoes wrapped in aluminum foil.

Jenny said,"Hank, Helen told me about the shooting in the rest area. I can't believe that someone could be that cruel and racist."

Hank said, "When you work in a police department for thirty two years, you come to realize that man can be the most dangerous animal on the planet. And mankind seems to be getting worse, not better."

Bill replied, "I think mankind appears to be getting worse because the population keeps growing; you still have the same percentage of bad apples."

"That may be true," Hank said. "Plus, with the almost instantaneous worldwide broadcast of the news, the bad news is always right up front."

"Bad news is a lot more profitable than good news," Bill replied. "Fronting the bad news is how papers and TV news stations stay in business. If our papers go out of business, Jenny's source of grocery coupons would dry up, along with Helen's daily crossword puzzles."

Helen said, "Hmm, just like a breeze off the African desert can develop into a hurricane and ravage the Gulf Coast, my daily crossword addiction may someday result in the downfall of mankind."

Bill laughingly said, "I think we all have to think about that one for awhile. Let's all have another beer and get these steaks and potatoes on the grill."

While loading up the grill, Bill paused and said, "Helen, can I use that in my weekly column?"

****

The Morans left Indianapolis mid-morning of the next day after repeated thanks to the Anspachs for the enjoyable visit. Bill made them promise to keep him abreast of their adventures as he needed more material for his Sunday travel column.

Their next planned stop was Grabill, Indiana, just fifteen miles north of Fort Wayne. Helen had read that Grabill was a small town in Allen County and was home to a fairly large settlement of Amish that had migrated to the area from Stark County, Ohio in 1853. Helen couldn't wait to get there; she thought it admirable how the Amish held true to their beliefs while the whole world changed around them. She also thought it was curious that the Allen County Amish carriages are open, while the Amish in Lancaster County, Pennsylvania ride in enclosed carriages. She hoped to gain an answer to that question in Grabill.

They were traveling north on Interstate 69 just south of Fort Wayne when Helen yelled, "Hank, pull over! I just saw a burned out pickup truck down off the highway!"

"Are you sure, Helen? I didn't see it," Hank replied.

"It's behind a small stand of trees down off the road. I just caught a glimpse of it as we drove by. We better stop and check it out in case somebody is hurt."

There was a wide berm on the highway, and Hank was able to safely pull over. They both walked back the hundred yards to where Helen saw the burned vehicle. They found it down off the highway behind trees nearly obscured from the road.

The vehicle was a burned out '07 GMC Sierra pickup. Small areas of the body still showed dark green paint. No bodies were in the cab. Hank saw the circles on the cracked back window where some decals were burned off in the fire. Faint outlines of lightning bolts were visible on the glass. No license tag was on the truck. The front bumper plate holder was also bare.

Hank dialed the number for Officer Bricker of the Indiana State Police. He told the officer he was sure he found the vehicle that was driven by the shooter two days ago in the rest area south of Indianapolis.

Officer Bricker was on the scene within the hour. He stated that no one had reported the fire. He had checked with the local and state dispatchers.

Helen remarked, "How can it be possible that the fire wasn't reported?"

Officer Bricker replied, "The fire was probably late at night with very little traffic on the highway, and besides, people just don't want to get involved anymore. Since it was so far off the road, passing motorists might have thought it was just a farmer burning tree trimmings. We were very lucky you spotted it, Mrs. Moran."

"Why would they burn their truck?"

"Mrs. Moran, many of the white supremacists are ex-military. Their fingerprints would be on file. They most likely burned the truck to destroy their DNA and fingerprints."

Helen asked, "Hank, how do we keep getting involved in these things?"

Hank replied, "Bill Anspach asked the same thing yesterday. I told him we were just lucky."

Officer Bricker discovered the VIN numbers were missing from both the door jamb and the dashboard. "Looks like they did a thorough job of removing all of the evidence. It's going to be difficult to track down the owner."

"There's probably around a thousand trucks like that registered in Michigan. You're going to have to get lucky to find a match," Hank replied.

"It wouldn't be so bad, but with the recent budget cuts, we are shorthanded."

"Well, like I said, you might get lucky."

Chapter 2

Officer Bricker once again thanked the Morans for their help, and told them to be very careful during the walk back to their motorhome. He offered them a ride, but Hank said it was OK for them to walk, as the officer was needed to control traffic around the scene. Traffic was already backing up with the closing of the right lane. The tow truck was slowly making its way up the bank to the highway. The burned out pickup, riding on its wheel rims, was securely fastened atop the flatbed of the wrecker truck.

Traffic was moving slowly and Hank was able to ease the Bounder back onto the highway with no problem. They were anxious to reach the campground in Fort Wayne and have a relaxed evening so they could explore the Amish country bright and early the next morning.

Helen was anxious to begin her quest of finding an answer to the question of why the Allen County Amish rode only in open buggies. Myriad Internet sites merely mentioned the fact, but none of them said why. Hank was amused by Helen's diligence and was looking forward to observing her investigative technique.

The Fort Wayne area was lacking in RV park selection. They happened to find a site available in the Johnny Appleseed Campground run by the City of Fort Wayne Parks and Recreation Department. The park was adequate for a short visit as it had only water and electric hook-ups available. Hank and Helen decided it would be just fine because of the large holding tanks in the Bounder. They could use the dump station on their way out in two days.

The next morning Helen took a quick shower, dressed, and was ready to drive the thirty miles up to Grabill. Hank was expecting breakfast, but Helen said they could eat a good country breakfast at the Grabill Inn Country Restaurant. She found out about the establishment from the campground host the night before. She thought it

14

would be a good place to start the search for answers to her questions about the Amish.

Approaching Grabill on Grabill Road the Morans slowed behind an Amish buggy with two women in the front seat and two rosy-cheeked girls facing the rear. The two young girls looked to be about five years old and waved when Hank eased past them with the Honda. Just a short distance down State Street to Fairview Drive and they were parking in the lot across the street from the restaurant.

Upon entering they were shown to one of the few remaining empty tables. Hank's eyes glazed over as he read the breakfast menu. He settled for the 'Old Farm' which was two eggs, home-fries, sausage, three silver dollar pancakes, toast, and coffee. He caught Helen looking at him and shaking her head. "I didn't know we were having guests," she said.

"What do you mean? I'm hungry," Hank replied. "It's halfway to lunch and I didn't have breakfast yet."

Helen settled for the cheese omelet, toast, and coffee.

When Hank's oversized platter arrived he dug in and didn't come up for air until his plate was clean. "Would you join me in a piece of apple pie?" he asked Helen.

"Hank! You've got to be kidding! We'll come back for desert after we walk around town for an hour or two."

When the waitress brought the check, Helen couldn't resist asking her if she knew why the Amish in the area rode in open buggies. The waitress said she had asked the same question when she arrived in town twenty three years ago and the only answer she received was "that's the way it's always been, it's part of their Ordnung."

Helen thanked her and Hank paid the check.

Helen knew from her research and earlier reading that the Ordnung were the rules of the church, or a blueprint of expected behavior, to which a particular Amish district adheres. She had read that the Ordnung is unwritten and the people just know it—as it is maintained by tradition and taught to the youth of the Order—and that the Ordnung is slow to change as the Order weighs the value of their forefathers decisions more heavily than passing fads.

Hank and Helen walked up State Street, peering in the windows of all the small quaint shops. They came across the Country Shops Antique Center. The Center had 30,000 square feet of antique furniture, glassware, and myriad odds and ends. Hank trudged through the store behind Helen, consoled with the knowledge that she would have to follow him around the Grabill Hardware Store of comparable size.

They reached Main Street and spied the Souder General Store just around the corner. Grabill Hardware was just across the street.

Helen said, "Let's check out the old general store first and then head across the street to the hardware."

Souder's was full of items unique to the Amish trade including solid color bolts of cloth, treadle type sewing machines, and button fly trousers. The only purchase the Morans made, however, was a bagful of locally made penny candy.

Upon exiting the general store Helen spotted the same two Amish ladies they had passed on Grabill Road. They were just getting into their buggy across the street at the hardware store. Helen rushed across the street with Hank following close behind.

"Excuse me, ladies," Helen said. "Could I ask you a question?"

One of the ladies dressed in a light blue dress and bonnet said with a German accent, "Yes. What do you want?"

"Excuse me for being so bold," Helen replied, "but I am trying to find the answer to a question I have had for some time. And that is, why do the Amish in this area ride only in open carriages?"

"It was decided long ago as part of our Ordnung. We do not question the reasons our forefathers made that decision. Perhaps you could ask our bishop. That is his carriage next to ours and he should be out in a minute."

Helen saw that one of the ladies had purchased a new cast iron fry pan. "Do they sell those fry pans in the hardware store?"

"Yes," the lady replied.

After the terse reply the driver snapped the reigns and the horse came to life and pulled the buggy from the parking lot. The two young girls sitting in back smiled and waved. Helen waved back.

Hank said, "Watch where you're stepping, Helen. Here comes the bishop. You can get your answer from the horse's mouth."

The bishop strode toward his buggy and noticed the Morans standing next to it.

"Hello, folks. Can I help you?"

"I was hoping you could. Are you the bishop?" Helen asked.

"Yes, I am Bishop Graber."

"I am Helen Moran and this is my husband, Hank."

Hank was impressed by the bishop's hardy and firm handshake.

"Now, what is it you wanted, Mrs. Moran?"

"I want to know why the Amish here in Allen County ride in open carriages and the Amish in Lancaster County, Pennsylvania use enclosed carriages."

"Mrs. Moran, we follow what is in the guidelines of our Ordnung. It was decided generations back to use open carriages. I don't want to second guess the wisdom of our forefathers, but I believe the main reason was to live as simple a life as possible. The plain carriage is just one of the ways to promote equality and unity in our community of equals. A simple carriage helps to prevent pride and envy. Plus we're not bashful and don't have to hide. Also we can look around at God's creation when we drive. Did I answer your question, Mrs. Moran?"

"Yes, you did, Bishop Graber. I appreciate you taking the time to talk with us."

And with that the bishop hopped up into his carriage and was on his way.

"They sure don't like to waste time," Hank said.

"Come on, Hank, let's go into the hardware store. I want to look at the cast iron fry pans."

"Are you going to upgrade your weapons arsenal?" Hank asked. He laughed as he remembered their maiden voyage over to Biloxi when she tried to bean an FBI agent with her large cast iron skillet.

Helen said, "I want to get a smaller fry pan. My skillet is just too big for the two of us for everyday use. The one the Amish lady bought looked like it was pre-seasoned. After the hardware store we can go get some of that dessert you so badly wanted."

"Sounds like a plan to me," Hank replied. "I've been thinking about some of that apple pie since we left the restaurant."

****

With Helen's question about the Amish carriages answered to her satisfaction, they spent the next day on a tour of the Fleetwood MotorHome manufacturing plant just down the road in Decatur, Indiana. They were impressed at the workmanship that went into Fleetwood's motorhomes. Much of the quality workmanship, they found out, was due to the high number of skilled Amish workers employed there.

The following morning they had all their things secured in the Bounder. Hank stopped at the campground's dump station and emptied the black and gray water tanks. They were on their way to Michigan. They planned an overnight stay in Lansing and then would head up to Mackinac the next day.

They lucked out and were able to get the last full hookup site available at the Cottonwood Campground in southern Lansing. While Hank was checking in at the desk Helen browsed through the rack full of pamphlets advertising local attractions. The brochure for the *Lansing Princess* riverboat caught her eye. They advertised a luncheon cruise on the Grand River, and Helen thought it would be a nice change of pace and a good way to relax for a day.

"Hank, register for two nights!" Helen excitedly said.

Hank told the clerk to change the reservation for two nights instead of one. He had learned not to question Helen's judgment when it came to things to do while traveling.

After they registered Hank asked Helen, "What did you find to do that you want to stay an additional night?"

"They have a riverboat cruise that sails over lunch, plus they have live music," Helen replied. "The boat is called the *Lansing Princess*. I just thought it would be a fun afternoon."

Hank commented, "I wonder what they have for dessert."

They found their site, and with practiced efficiency, had the Bounder hooked up to the utilities in short order. For dinner they decided to eat at the Dublin Square Irish Pub, which was recommended by the campground's clerk.

Hank enjoyed a mug full of Guinness and bangers—the pub served the grilled Irish sausages over sautéed red onions and roasted red peppers much to Hank's satisfaction—while Helen opted for the grilled salmon. For dessert Hank imbibed in another mug of Guinness. After dinner, Helen drove the Honda back to the campground as Hank recuperated in the passenger seat chewing antacids.

The next morning Hank was sent on a mission to the campground office to obtain the morning newspaper to sate Helen's crossword puzzle addiction. Helen liked to send him out while she prepared breakfast or else he would be hovering around her like a vulture. She thought retirement had begun stimulating his appetite.

Hank scanned the front page of the *Lansing State Journal* while walking back to the Bounder. He flipped the paper over to read the bottom half of page one and an article caught his eye. It wasn't necessarily the article's headline but the associated picture that caught his attention.

The article was about the discovery of a missing Waverly man's body in neighboring Barry County. The body had been found by a road maintenance crew just off Solomon Road near Black Lake. The man was identified as Jason Wengert. Barry County Sheriff, Bobby Engle, said it looked like Mr. Wengert was the victim of a hit-and-run driver.

Wengert's Michigan driver's license photo was printed beside the article. Hank studied the picture and thought he could make out a dark patch on Wengert's left cheek. He swore he was looking at a picture of the killer of Agusto Soto.

****

Six Days Earlier

Jason Wengert and Harry Griggs had just participated in a morning white power rally in Seymour, Indiana. It was Wengert's first out of state rally and he was still on a high when he sped onto the onramp for Interstate 65, just after noon. The beer he consumed after the rally was working its way through his system and he needed to relieve himself.

"There's a rest area just above Columbus. We can make a pit stop there," Griggs informed him. "It's only about twenty miles ahead."

"Good, I think I can hold out twenty miles without pissin my pants," Wengert replied.

Seventeen minutes later Wengert sped into the rest area and walked briskly to the men's room. It was crowded and he had to wait in line. He unfortunately entered behind a group from a tour bus and there were a few Hispanic men in front of him talking and joking with one another.

Wengert was starting to lose his cool and said, "Come on you guys, stop foolin around. There are people here waiting to go."

The men glanced his way and continued to converse. The only word Wengert caught was 'gringo.' He knew they were talking about him and it heightened his angry state. He finally found an empty stall and did his business.

Wengert left the men's room and trotted down to the end of the parking area to his truck.

Griggs asked, "What in hell took you so long? It's hotter than hell in here."

"There were some damn wetbacks jabbering and fooling around in there. They pissed me off."

Wengert reached over and took a 9mm Smith and Wesson MP from the glove compartment. "I'll show the bastards," he said, as he started up the truck and sped down the lot. He reached the rest rooms and stopped when he saw a Hispanic looking man standing beside a late model SUV. He opened the window, uttered "fuckin wetback," and fired twice at the man. He then sped toward the onramp to the interstate, narrowly missing an older man who barely managed to jump out of the way.

"What the hell did you do that for?" Griggs hollered.

"I told you they pissed me off."

"The major's not going to like this. In fact he's probably going to go off on one of his tirades. He had reservations about you from the beginning. The only reason he let you stay in the battalion was because of your old man."

"Well, fuck the major. Let him get pissed."

Griggs replied, "We're gonna have to ditch the truck. They'll be lookin for it before we hit Michigan. You can report it stolen to the sheriff when we get home."

Ninety miles later Griggs noticed the highway had an extra wide berm and told Wengert to slow down. "Look up ahead, there's a big stand of trees down off the road. Pull the damn truck down there behind the trees. I'll try to raise Carter and Jacobs on their cell. They should only be about a half hour behind us."

Wengert did as he was told. He was down off his high and was beginning to regret what he had done at the rest area. Griggs told him he would regret it a lot more when the major found out what he did.

Griggs managed to contact Carter and told him about the shooting. He gave him the mile marker and said for him to stop at the Wal-Mart at the exit below them.

"Get a can of gas and a couple large candles. Then come and pick us up."

While they were waiting for Carter and Jacobs the two men busied themselves with removing the truck's license tag and VIN plates from the door and dash. They had to break the windshield in order to work loose the plate on the dash. Griggs reminded Wengert to remove the MSU tag from the front bumper.

Forty-five minutes later Carter and Jacobs pulled up behind them.

"You got the gas and candles?" Griggs asked.

"Yeah, we've got five gallons of gas and a box with three candles," Carter replied.

"That's good. That should do just fine."

Griggs punched holes in the front and rear seats with his hunting knife and stuck in the three candles so that five inches of each candle was left protruding. He doused the exterior of the truck with gasoline and poured a generous amount on the seats and floor carpet. After waiting for the fumes to clear he carefully lit the three candles.

"What's with the candles?" Wengert asked.

"The candles will burn down at about an inch per hour. By the time the truck gets torched this evening we should be at home and in bed with our old ladies," Griggs replied. "Let's get the hell out of here now."

"Oh man, now I'm gonna lose my truck. All because of some fuckin wetbacks," Wengert lamented.

"No, it's because of your fuckin stupidity," Griggs replied.

The next day Griggs stopped in at the major's farm near the small town of Dowling, Michigan.

"Griggs, what in hell got into Wengert yesterday? I had you ride with him to keep him under control," the major bellowed.

"Major, he did just fine until on the way home from the rally. Some Mexicans pissed him off at the rest area, and before I could stop him he pulled a gun out of the glove box and started firing."

"Griggs, the kid is a loose cannon. We can't have him screwing up our plans. If the damned cops find out he was the shooter it'll draw too much attention our way. He needs to be eliminated."

Chapter 3

Hank walked briskly back to the motorhome with Helen's newspaper. Upon entering the Bounder he began a search for his cell phone.

"Helen, did you see my cell phone anywhere?"

"I think you left it up front on the console between the seats. Why do you need your cell phone? Breakfast is ready."

"Look at the front page of the newspaper I just brought in. That hit-and-run victim looks just like the guy who shot Agusto Soto. I can even make out the birthmark on his left cheek."

"Well then, you better call Officer Bricker. I can keep your breakfast warm for a little while."

Hank retrieved his cell phone from the front console. Bricker's card was still in the console beside the phone. Hank punched in Bricker's number and the officer answered on the second ring.

"Officer Dan Bricker speaking."

"Officer Bricker, this is Hank Moran. I have something additional to report on the Agusto Soto shooting.

"Good morning, Mr. Moran. Did you remember the tag number on the pickup truck?"

"I can do better than that. Can you get a copy of this morning's *Lansing State Journal*? I am at least ninety-five percent certain the shooter's picture is on the front page. He was a victim of a hit-and-run accident, or so says Barry County Sheriff, Bobby Engle."

"I can't lay my hands on that paper right away. I'll have to locate it on the Internet. You sound skeptical about the hit-and-run, Mr. Moran."

"If this is the shooter it just seems a little too coincidental. His name is Jason Wengert and he lived in Waverly. It might be worth your while to check with the Michigan DMV to see if he owned a green '07 Sierra like the one we found burned out alongside the highway. Oh, and I can make out what looks like the birthmark I said I saw on his left cheek."

"Are you still in the area, Mr. Moran?"

"Well, no, we are up in Lansing."

"That's even better. How long do you plan to stay up there?"

"We planned to stay two nights and then head up to the Upper Peninsula."

"Mr. Moran, let me check on this guy's vehicle registration. If it pans out that he owns the truck I will take a run up there today. I'd like you to go with me to the morgue that handles Barry County to take a better look at this guy."

"Well, we had plans to go on a riverboat cruise over lunch, but we are flexible. Call me back after you check his vehicle registration. If this helps to find the shooter my wife will be more than willing to postpone our plans."

"I'll call you back as soon as possible. Thanks for your help, Mr. Moran."

"No thanks necessary, Officer. I'll be expecting your call."

"OK, Helen, I'm ready to dig in to that breakfast now."

"Hank, what is it with you and your appetite lately? You've been eating like a horse on this whole trip."

"Helen, it has to be because of my retirement. After thirty years on the force, I'm finally starting to relax. I'm really starting to enjoy my food. When I was working, eating was just something I did to keep up the energy on my job. I had to grab meals whenever I could. I knew there was something out there better than doughnuts and pizza, but I didn't have the time to find out."

"Tell me about it," Helen said. "I couldn't count the number of times I cooked us dinner, only to have to sit and eat by myself when you were called out on an emergency investigation."

"Well, sweetheart, you won't have to eat alone anymore. Just keep cookin.'"

"Yeah, I'm going to have to learn how to cook light, or else you're going to need a whole new wardrobe."

"Promise me you won't do that until I have to loosen my belt a notch."

An hour later, Officer Bricker returned Hank's call.

"Mr. Moran, it looks like you were right about Wengert. There is a green 2007 GMC Sierra registered to Jason Wengert of Waverly, Michigan. The body is presently at the morgue in Lansing. I notified Sheriff Engle of Barry County that we will be IDing the body. I am flying up there in the state police bird and can meet you at the morgue in two hours. It's located in the Medical Arts Building on East Michigan Avenue."

"We'll find it, Officer. See you in two hours."

"Hank, you said *we* will find it. Does that mean I can go along?"

"Helen, do you mean you want to look at a dead body?"

"Well, I am not too keen on looking at a dead body, but I'm just beginning to get the chance to see firsthand, what your job was like the last thirty years. I find it interesting to experience what you experienced."

"I assure you it won't be fun looking at the victim of a hit-and-run. If you think you can handle it you're welcome to come along."

Hank and Helen arrived at the Medical Arts Building five minutes early. They were approaching the receptionist's counter when Officer Bricker came through the door.

Bricker approached the couple and extended his hand.

"Mr. and Mrs. Moran, I see you had no problem finding the building."

"No problem at all," Hank said as he shook Bricker's hand.

Bricker then lightly shook Helen's hand.

"Well, folks, let's go pay a visit to Mr. Wengert."

The receptionist called ahead to the coroner's office then informed the group, "Coroner Holcomb is waiting for you in the morgue. Just go down the hall and take the elevator one flight down. The morgue is just off the elevator to the right."

25

When they exited the elevator Hank looked around and said, "Helen, there is a ladies' room just across the hall from the morgue entrance."

"That's OK, I don't have to go," Helen replied.

"It's just for your future reference."

Hank smiled as they entered the morgue. The morgue was not as bad as Hank was accustomed to. It had an antiseptic smell but the odor of death was minimal. Coroner Holcomb introduced himself and told the small group to follow him. He stopped in front of a bank of stainless steel drawers and selected number eight.

Holcomb pulled open the drawer to reveal the form of a body under a white sheet.

"Do you folks wish to view the entire body?" Holcomb asked.

Bricker replied, "I think we only need to make a facial ID. Am I right, Mr. Moran?"

"I think that will do," Hank replied.

Coroner Holcomb folded the white sheet down to below Wengert's chin saying, "He's not a pretty sight. He must have been lying out there a few days. The birds got to his eyes."

The first thing Hank noticed was the large red birthmark on Wengert's left cheek. Wengert had multiple contusions on his face and forehead with accompanying discoloration. It was hard to distinguish between the actual injuries and the work of the birds. The empty eye sockets were a gruesome sight. Hank was able to make a positive ID based on the color of hair and the unique birthmark.

Hank turned to see how Helen was coping and just caught a glimpse of her through the closing morgue door as she was heading across the hall to the ladies' room.

"Well, thank you for all your help, Mr. Moran," Bricker said. "It feels good to have this case closed so fast. I am going to have to report my findings to Sheriff Engle and I am sure he will want to talk with you."

"That's fine," Hank replied. "I assume you are also going to contact Mrs. Soto with the news?"

"Yes I will, Mr. Moran. In fact I am also going to show her Wengert's driver's license photo. I don't think I'll confront her with the shots from the morgue. A dual verification that Wengert was the shooter will be more than enough to close the case."

"Well, Coroner Holcomb, Officer Bricker, I better go track down my wife. I saw her heading to the ladies' room."

Helen was exiting the ladies' room as Hank was coming out of the morgue.

"Are you OK, Helen?"

"Well, I was OK until I saw that guy's face. The odors in there weren't that bad, but when the coroner pulled that sheet down and I saw Wengert's face with the empty eye sockets I started to feel a little woozy."

"Are you OK now?"

"Yes, I'm just fine. A little cold water on my face did the trick."

"Well, Helen, you did a lot better than me on my first morgue experience. Let's just say I couldn't keep things in place, if you know what I mean. Although viewing an autopsy is a little more intense than just making an ID."

"Holy cow, Hank! I never realized that some of the things you had to endure were so bad."

"Some things I never brought home. I left a lot of the bad stuff at the office."

"You poor dear."

"Sheriff Engle, this is Officer Dan Bricker from Indiana calling you back."

"Go ahead, Officer."

"The witness, Mr. Hank Moran, just made a positive ID of Wengert as the shooter down in the rest area in Indiana. As far as I am concerned the case is closed at our end, unless you can uncover who was riding with Wengert."

"Bricker, it might be difficult to prove accessory to murder just because the guy was a passenger in Wengert's truck, especially with Wengert dead."

"You're right, Sheriff, I don't think there was a conspiracy to commit either. A number of witnesses at the scene claim there was a flare-up in the men's room between Wengert and some Hispanics just before the shooting."

"Did anyone actually see the passenger well enough to ID him?"

"No, not at all. Apparently the passenger waited in the truck while Wengert went inside to use the facilities. The best the witnesses could come up with was that he looked older than the shooter."

"Bricker, how sure are you of this Moran's ID of Wengert?"

"Sheriff, he was one hundred percent certain as he had a good look at Wengert's birthmark as he drove by him in the truck. He is a recently retired homicide detective from Louisiana with over thirty years' experience. He knows the importance of getting things correct in these matters."

"Well, a birthmark like that is one in a million. I guess this wraps it up for you then. Give me Moran's number just in case I decide to have a chat with him."

Bricker gave Hank's phone number to Sheriff Engle, and before ending the call he asked, "Sheriff Engle, one more thing. Soto was shot with a nine millimeter. I would like to search Wengert's place for a handgun. If we find one I would like to do a ballistics test on it just for further confirmation. I can stop over there before I head back home if you have the time to assist me."

"No problem. Come on over. I'll have a search warrant ready for when you get here."

Sheriff Engle hung up the receiver, paused a moment, then picked it up again and dialed. "Major, this is Engle."

"Yes, Engle. How is our illustrious sheriff today?"

"Doing well, Major. I just got off the phone with the Indiana state cop. His witness made a positive ID of Wengert right down to his damned birthmark. From what I understand Indiana is going to consider the case closed. They are not going to try to determine who was riding with Wengert. The state cop went along with my suggestion that it was a 'heat of the moment' reaction from Wengert. It would be impossible to prove any complicity on the part of the passenger in any kind of premeditation. Especially with Wengert not being able to talk. He requested for me to aid in the search for Wengert's gun. I told him it wouldn't be a problem."

"Sounds like you did well, Sheriff. What about the witness? Any chance of trouble from him?"

"I doubt it, Major. He and his wife were traveling through the area in a motorhome, and I suspect they will be moving on. The thing is, though, he is a recently retired homicide detective from Louisiana."

"Shit, Engle, why don't you give him a call just to find out his intentions? Keep it entirely businesslike. Just don't stir anything up!"

"Will do, Major."

Hank's phone rang just as he and Helen were returning to their motorhome from the morgue. He put the call on the speaker phone.

"Hello, this is Hank Moran."

"Mr. Moran, this is Sheriff Bobby Engle from Barry County. I understand from Officer Bricker that you made a positive ID of Wengert as the shooter down in the Indiana rest area. We appreciate your help in settling the matter."

"Just doing my civic duty, Sheriff. I was glad to help."

"Well, I just wanted to call to let you know we appreciate your help. It is always encouraging to have a citizen stand up and do the right thing. I understand you are traveling through the area in a motorhome. The wife and I have been thinking about buying one when I retire."

"I think you would enjoy it, Sheriff. We certainly do. We are on our way up to the Upper Peninsula, then plan to head into Canada."

"Then you will be pulling out soon, I suspect?"

"We plan to stay in Lansing one more day to do a riverboat cruise, then we will be heading north. Oh, Sheriff, there is something that has been bothering me about Wengert."

"What is that, Mr. Moran?"

"Are you positive that Wengert's death was a hit-and-run? It just seems odd that he would be the victim of an accident like that so shortly after the shooting in Indiana."

"I don't know what you mean by odd, Mr. Moran. Accidents can happen at any time. That's why they are called accidents. I see no need for you to concern yourself about it. The preliminary medical examiner's report said Wengert's injuries were consistent with being hit by a fast moving auto."

"Yes, I know, Officer Bricker said the same thing. Oh, another thing, Sheriff, do you know if Wengert belonged to a white power group?"

"Hell, half the men in rural Michigan belong to one group or another, Mr. Moran. The NRA and gun rights are big things up here."

"I know, Sheriff, I gathered as much from the Internet. I understand that Michigan has nearly as many fringe groups as the leader, Texas, but with one third the population."

"Well there you go, Mr. Moran. It looks like you answered your own question. Well, I'd like to continue to chat about our lovely state up here, but I have a busy schedule today. Enjoy the rest of your stay in Michigan, and have a safe trip to the U.P."

"Thank you, Sheriff, we'll surely try. Goodbye."

Helen listened to the sheriff's call on the speaker phone, then questioned Hank:

"Hank, what do you make of the sheriff's call?"

"Well, I don't think he called just to thank us. I got the impression that he was feeling us out as to our intentions. I don't think he wants us hanging around the area."

"Are we going to hang around Lansing for awhile?"

"Let's just see how tomorrow goes. I'm looking forward to the riverboat cruise. Maybe afterward we can decide what to do."

"Hank, do you still feel that Wengert's death wasn't accidental?"

"That's my gut feeling, Helen, but we bought a motorhome to go traveling and to see the country. Do we really want to get involved with another investigation? I have a feeling these guys up here play a little rough. This is a little different than having a whole police force behind you."

"OK, let's see what tomorrow brings."

After his call to Hank, Sheriff Engle reported back to the major.

"Major, Engle again. I just got off the phone with the guy who identified Wengert. They are going to be in the

30

area for one more day and then head north. They plan to take the lunchtime river cruise on the *Princess* tomorrow. I don't know if he is going to poke around, but he did have the balls to ask if I was sure the hit-and-run was accidental."

"What would make him question that?"

"He just said it was an odd sequence of events with Wengert being the shooter and then dying in an accident. I assured him it was an accident."

"Well, what's the guy's name?"

"His name is Hank Moran."

"I'll have to take a lunchtime cruise tomorrow on the *Lansing Princess* and make it a point to meet Mr. and Mrs. Moran. Keep me informed if anything else transpires with regards to Mr. Wengert's *accident*."

"Will do, Major."

Chapter 4

The following morning Hank went on his regular morning quest to buy a copy of the local newspaper while Helen prepared breakfast. When he entered the camp store the clerk said, "Good morning, Mr. Moran. It's kinda neat having a celebrity staying at the campground."

Hank responded, "I'm sure it is ma'am. Who's the celebrity?"

"Why, you are," the clerk replied. "You're in the morning paper."

"How so?"

"There's an article on the second page of the front section about how you identified that Wengert character as the guy who shot the Mex down in Indiana."

"I am sorry, ma'am, but the gentleman who was shot was not a 'Mex.' He was a US citizen with a college degree."

The clerk raised her eyebrows but didn't respond verbally. Hank could tell the clerk was holding back, clearly not wanting to get into a debate about the illegal immigration issue. Hank was glad, as he did not want to debate the issue either. He paid for the newspaper and left the store.

Hank and Helen were walking from their Honda towards the *Lansing Princess* dock when they came upon a black Escalade with tinted windows. Hank glanced at the back of the large SUV and noticed a dual lightning bolt decal on the rear window. "Helen, look at that," Hank said as he pointed to the decal. "It looks like one of our friendly white supremacists is going on the cruise with us."

"Hank, write down that tag number in your notebook. Maybe Gerry could tell us who it belongs to."

"Good idea, but I hate to bother my old partner again until we have a real good reason."

Hank wrote down the tag number in his notebook, then proceeded to the boat dock with Helen on his arm. There was a short line of people waiting to board the *Princess* as the captain was personally greeting all boarders. He was of medium height and slender, decked out in his white captain's suit with the traditional epaulets and black brimmed white cap.

"Welcome aboard the *Lansing Princess*. I am Captain Winston Kerr, and you are?"

"We are Hank and Helen Moran."

Upon hearing Hank's introduction to the captain, the man preceding the Morans onto the boat turned and glanced at Hank and Helen then walked on.

"Ahh, from south Louisiana I bet. New Orleans area."

"Very good, Captain. How could you tell?" Hank asked.

"I've been greeting passengers aboard the *Princess* for twenty three years and have become quite good at distinguishing the nuances in my guests' speech. You do have a slight Cajun flavor in yours, Mr. Moran, which would place you in southern Louisiana rather than farther north. But you also have the Brooklyn sounding accent from New Orleans."

"I am impressed with your ability, Captain Kerr. I hope your lunch buffet is just as impressive."

"I am sure you will find that our buffet exceeds all your expectations, Mr. Moran. Ms. Reed, our hostess, will direct you to the Grand Salon. The dinner bell will sound once we are underway."

While the boat was preparing to get underway, Hank and Helen decided to explore the one hundred and ten foot, triple deck craft. They made their way through the elegant Grand Salon, which had seating for one-hundred-eighty guests, to the stairs leading to the second and third decks. The second deck had seating for over two-hundred in multiple rooms. The third and upper deck contained the wheelhouse and the captain's dining room, which seated sixty guests. There was also a generous amount of seating in the open-air section of the third deck.

Hank and Helen paused at the handrail on the upper deck and gazed at the swirling waters of the Grand River nearly thirty feet below. "Looks like they have plenty of life preservers," Hank said as he peered down the promenade.

"They might need them. This section of handrail seems a little shaky."

"Come on, Hank. Be more optimistic. We're here for lunch, not a swim," Helen replied.

"Helen, remember, I was a Boy Scout. Our motto was 'Be Prepared.' Hey, I feel the boat moving."

With the muffled sound of the thrusters the *Lansing Princess* sidled away from the dock. Thirty feet out into the river the main engine engaged and the luncheon cruise was underway.

Hank and Helen made it back down to the Grand Salon just as the dinner bell sounded. With a little luck and perfect timing, they were third in line at the generous buffet. Helen opted to start out with a salad. The good example she tried to set was unnoticed by Hank as he piled his plate with fried chicken, barbecued beans, and potato salad.

Being near the head of the line had its advantage as they had their pick of tables and found an empty one along the side next to a window. As they were enjoying their first course, a man approached their table with his plate in hand. He was about the same height as Hank with graying hair that was trimmed in a short military style flat top. He looked about fifty years of age but had the toned body of a much younger man.

"Mind if I join you?" the man asked.

"Be our guest, pull up a chair," Hank replied. "The table seats six."

"Thank you. I'm Walter Duesterbeck."

"Glad to meet you, Walter. I'm Hank Moran, and this is my wife, Helen."

"Hmm, Hank Moran. I'm trying to recall where I just heard your name."

"Perhaps you heard our introduction to the captain upon boarding," Helen said. "You were in front of us and turned when you heard our names."

That's true, Mrs. Moran, but I think I saw your name before that. That's why I turned."

"Did you read the morning paper?" Hank asked. "Page two?"

"Yes, that's it! You are the person who identified the body of that hit-and-run victim as the gunman down in Indiana."

"Yes, that was me," Hank replied "An unfortunate sequence of tragic events."

"That must have been a disquieting interruption to your travel plans. The paper said you were traveling through the area in your motorhome when the shooting occurred."

"We were on our way to visit some friends in Indianapolis and just happened to take a break at the rest area. Hank just wanted to stop for a state map," Helen offered.

"Well, Mrs. Moran, life does have its twists and turns."

"Gentlemen, you'll have to excuse me while I return to the buffet line," Helen said. "I finished my salad and now I am going to try a piece of that fried chicken."

Duesterbeck rose from his chair when Helen stood up to leave the table.

"You have an adorable wife, Mr. Moran. Unfortunately, I lost mine a few years ago."

"Well, thank you, Mr. Duesterbeck. I am sorry to hear of your loss."

"Like I said earlier, life does have its twists and turns. And, please, call me Walter. My last name is quite cumbersome."

"Will do, Walter, please call me Hank."

"The paper said you were a recently retired homicide detective. It must be a little disconcerting to retire from an occupation such as that only to have tragedy follow you."

"Well, Walter, in a way it is, but I was also able to be of service to the community in helping to solve the case. What do you do for a living?"

"I guess you could call me a gentlemen farmer. I have a four hundred acre farm over near Dowling. I lease a few hundred acres out to a real farmer, and on the rest I have a quail and pheasant habitat. I am an avid small game hunter, especially the birds. I inherited the farm from my father. When I retired from the Marine Corp I decided to make it my home. My mother still lives there. She enjoys living on the farm so I decided to hang on to it, at least until she passes on."

"What was your rank when you retired?"

"I retired as a major. What was your rank on the police force?

"I made my way up to Detective Lieutenant from Patrolman. It looks like you outrank me, Walter."

"Not hardly, Hank. We are comparing apples and oranges. Did you serve in the military?"

"I spent four years in the army and then took up civil engineering on the GI Bill."

"I'm confused. How did you go from civil engineering to the police?"

"I found engineering too boring. Spent six months at the police academy and the rest is history. As you said. Life has its twists and turns."

Helen returned to the table with her piece of fried chicken, coleslaw, and a small amount of baby carrots and pickled beets.

Duesterbeck said he saw some friends at another table waving at him to go over. "Well folks, I hope you enjoy the rest of your stay in Michigan. Will you be leaving Lansing in the morning?"

Helen replied, "That's our plan. We hope to make it to the Upper Peninsula tomorrow. That is if nothing further develops with that supposed hit-and-run situation."

Duesterbeck suddenly looked alarmed. "What did you mean about Wengert's hit-and-run?"

"My husband and I both think there is something more to it besides an accidental hit-and-run case."

"Well folks, I wouldn't let it bother you. You seem like very nice people and you should just enjoy the rest of your trip. I am sure the area police did all they could do. Now, if you will excuse me I need to pay a visit to some friends."

When Duesterbeck left the table Helen said, "Did you notice the alarmed look on his face when I questioned the hit-and-run?"

"Yes, I did. And did you notice how all of a sudden he brought up Wengert's name? Earlier he just called him 'that hit-and-run victim.'"

"You're right, Hank! Could it be there was an ulterior motive in Mr. Duesterbeck's visit to our table?"

"I'm beginning to think so. I think we should find out just who Mr. Duesterbeck is."

The entertainment aboard the riverboat started just as the buffet was winding down. The music being produced by one man and a keyboard amazed the Morans. For the next hour Hank and Helen danced while the boat made its way back to the dock. When the boat was safely moored Captain Kerr was once again at the ramp wishing everyone a good day as they departed the *Lansing Princess*. As Hank approached the captain he mentioned the loose handrail on the upper deck.

"Thank you for informing me about that, Mr. Moran," Captain Kerr said. "I will surely have it checked out."

The black Escalade was just backing out of its parking space when Hank and Helen walked by on their return to their Honda. Duesterbeck waved as he pulled away.

"Well, Helen, I guess we now know who the friendly white supremacist is."

The Morans had a decision to make when they returned to their Bounder motorhome. "Well, should we pull out in the morning and head up to the U.P. or stick around here for another day?" Hank asked.

"Well, dear, I have a feeling we should extend our stay at least a couple more days. We could contact Bill Anspach and see if he could do some research on Mr. Duesterbeck. His researcher sure dug up all the goodies on our old preacher friend last month."

"You're right.It might take a whole day for her to come up with the information. I'll call Bill right away and then walk down to the office and extend our stay."

Hank found his cell phone on the front console of the Bounder and punched in Bill's number.

Upon recognizing Hank's number he answered. "Hello, Hank, you must be calling with some new material for my column."

"It could very well lead to that, Bill, but first I wonder if you could get your researcher to do some more work for us. I believe her name was Mary Sue?"

"Perhaps I can, Hank. What did you do? Run into another serial murder situation?"

"Well, I hope it doesn't develop into that. Right now it's just a questionable hit-and-run case. And it might involve some local white supremacist. This is all connected with the shooting of Agusto Soto."

"OK, just what do you need? I'll see if I can help."

"I need some information on a Walter Duesterbeck. He owns a farm near Dowling, Michigan. He drives a black Escalade with white power decals on the back window. We met him on a riverboat luncheon cruise today. Both Helen and I think the meeting wasn't by chance. I think he was seeking us out."

"Why would he do that, Hank?"

"I questioned the sheriff in Jason Wengert's hit-and-run case as to whether he was sure it was actually an accident. He got a little upset and basically encouraged us to continue along on our journey. Now this Duesterbeck suggested the same thing when Helen told him that we have the legitimacy of the hit-and-run in question. Now my old intuition is at work thinking there is some connection between the sheriff and Duesterbeck. Oh, and I did tell the sheriff we were taking the luncheon riverboat cruise. I think that is how Duesterbeck knew to find us there."

"I'll tell you what, Hank. I have an acquaintance on the *Lansing State Journal*. His passion is writing about the white power groups up in Michigan. If there is anything to know about this Duesterbeck fellow, he would be the guy to talk to. His name is Rolf Kramden. I'll give him a call to see if he will talk to you. One of us will call you back shortly."

"Thanks, Bill, I really appreciate your help."

After hanging up from Bill, Hank walked down to the park office to extend their stay for an additional two days. After carefully checking the campground booking schedule the clerk gave them the OK. As Hank was walking back to the Bounder, Helen met him with his cell phone in hand.

"Hank, you have a phone call. It's the guy from the newspaper."

Helen handed the phone to Hank. "Hello, this is Hank Moran."

"Hello, Mr. Moran, this is Rolf Kramden from the *Journal*. Bill Anspach said you needed some information on Walter Duesterbeck."

"Greetings, Mr. Kramden. Please, call me Hank. I would appreciate anything you have on the guy."

"I have quite a lot, Hank. Is there some place we can meet? I have some clippings you might be interested in seeing. Bill Anspach said you are a retired homicide detective and were instrumental in solving that preacher related series of murders over in Tennessee and Mississippi. He said you might be on to something with the Wengert hit-and-run."

"That is correct, Rolf. I don't know where we could meet as we are not familiar with the area. We are staying in a motorhome at the Cottonwood Campground in southern Lansing."

"Tell you what, Hank. I live about a mile away from the campground. Is it possible to meet at your motorhome? I've always wanted to see the inside of one of those rigs."

"Sure thing, Rolf. We are just down from the entrance in a gold and black Bounder. A gray Honda is parked in front."

"See you in about an hour then, Hank. I'll gather up some material and stop there on my way home."

"See you then, Rolf."

One hour later, as promised, Rolf Kramden rolled into the campground in his blue Prius and parked beside the Honda. Hank and Helen were sitting outside under the awning in their lawn chairs and watched as Kramden extricated his lanky six foot frame from the small hybrid.

"Hello, folks, I'm Rolf Kramden."

"Hank and Helen Moran," Hank responded as they shook hands, "Please, have a seat."

"It's a pleasure to meet you folks. I was the reporter who wrote the story of Hank IDing Wengert as the shooter down in the Indiana rest area. I hope I had everything correct in the story."

"I think you covered all the bases. What is your take on the hit-and-run?" Hank asked.

"Well, like you, I thought something sounded a little fishy about the so-called accident. I started thinking that there must be something more to the story. Let's go over what I have on Duesterbeck, then we can take it from there."

"Sounds like the right tactic, Rolf. What have you got?"

"OK. To start with, Duesterbeck is a retired Marine major. He served long enough to leave the Corp with a healthy pension. He retired about five years ago. About the same time his father passed away and left him a sizable farm over near Dowling. The stipulation of the will stated that Walter's mother was to live on the farm until such time that she passes on. His mother is worth a considerable amount in stocks and bonds, so it was prudent for Walter to agree to the stipulations of the will."

"It appears he is pretty well set for life," Hank said.

"That he is. Now to get to the interesting part. About four years ago he joined a group called the Conservative Citizens Battalion. Being a former Marine major he was heartily welcomed into the group. The Battalion founder was none other than William Wengert; who was the father of Jason Wengert."

"You speak of William Wengert in the past tense."

"That's right. William died of heart failure two years ago. And guess who was made Commander of the Conservative Citizens Battalion."

"Walter Duesterbeck!" Hank and Helen answered in unison.

"So what's with this Conservative Citizens Battalion?" Hank asked. "It sounds kind of benign to me."

"That group has always stayed under the radar. From what I can tell, they like to play war games out on Duesterbeck's farm. You know with paintball guns and all. He erected a good sized shooting range and a few false front buildings where they can practice street type combat. There have been a few complaints of automatic weapons fire from the closest neighbor, but the sheriff has always downplayed it."

"Let me guess. The sheriff is Bobby Engle."

"You are right, Hank. Our Mr. Duesterbeck was a major contributor to Engle's re-election campaign and I would think he has quite a bit more influence with the sheriff than the average citizen."

Helen asked, "Did Sheriff Engle ever participate in the war games?"

"I only heard rumors to that effect. Nothing I could substantiate to put in writing," Rolf replied. "Now, there is something I need to show you," he said as he pulled a folder from his valise.

"These are photos from the white power rally down in Seymour, Indiana, the morning Mr. Soto was murdered. I was able to get digital copies of the photos and printed them out on larger paper. This first photo has a good shot of Jason Wengert," Rolf said as he handed it to Hank. "Please look at the guys around Wengert and see if you recognize any of them as the passenger in Wengert's truck."

"I didn't get a very good look at him as I was trying to get out of the way of the truck, Hank replied. "I did notice that he looked older than Wengert. My impression was he was probably in his fifties."

"OK, Hank, here's another pic of the group. Look at the guy just to the left of Wengert and see if he jogs your memory."

"The guy does look about the right age. Wait! Now I do recall the long mustache. It may very well be the guy that was riding shotgun."

"Great!" Rolf replied. "That is Mr. Harry Griggs. He is one of Duesterbeck's top lieutenants. He may even be second in command of the Battalion."

"Rolf, let's get back to the hit-and-run. What was Wengert doing out that late at night, on foot, on an isolated road?

"He supposedly went up there with two of his friends, namely Harry Griggs and Dan Carter, to spot deer. It's a normal thing to do prior to the opening of deer season."

"Isn't it a little early for that activity?" Hank asked.

"Well, the antlerless season starts in late September. An avid hunter would start spotting for deer trails about now," Rolf replied.

"If he went up there with two friends how did he manage to get hit? How did the whole thing supposedly happen?" Hank asked.

"According to Sheriff Engle, Griggs drove and dropped Wengert and Carter off about two hundred yards apart. Then he proceeded about another two hundred yards. Supposedly they kept in touch with walkie-talkies. About two and a half hours later, Griggs told Carter and Wengert to make their way back to the road so he could pick them up. Griggs picked up Carter first and then started looking for Wengert. They tried to raise him on the walkie-talkie but got no response. Griggs drove up and down the road for a half mile in either direction from where he dropped Wengert off but saw no sign of him. They then figured he got a ride with somebody else and left. They said Wengert told them that some friends might come up to help out. The rest is history. Oh, and Carter said an old red Ford truck passed him at a high rate of speed while he was waiting for Griggs to pick him up."

"How convenient. Did they check Griggs' truck for any damage?" Helen asked.

"Good question. I asked Engle the same thing, and he said Griggs' truck was clean. Engle figured Wengert saw the approaching truck, thinking it was Griggs, and stepped out to flag him down. The driver of the red truck didn't see him in time and nailed him."

Hank asked, "Did the sheriff have any luck in locating the mysterious red truck?"

"All he would say is that it is an ongoing investigation."

"Yeah, and I bet it's at the very bottom of the sheriff's priority list," Hank replied. "I sure would like to get a look at Griggs' truck."

"I can save you the trouble," Rolf replied. "I followed Griggs to the Wal-Mart over in Hastings this morning and had a chance to inspect the front end of his truck while he was inside the store. He has a heavy duty chrome deer guard mounted on the front end. The whole truck looked spotless, and nothing appeared bent or damaged on the front end."

"Looks like you did a thorough job in your investigation," Hank said.

"Just a normal day in the life of an investigative reporter," Rolf replied.

"Damn, it still bothers me that both Engle and Duesterbeck seemed to get defensive when I questioned the veracity of the hit-and-run accident," Hank said. "Let's go inside the coach and pop open a few beers and do some brainstorming."

Rolf was visibly impressed with the interior of the Bounder. "Wow, I could live in a rig like this," he exclaimed as he looked around.

"Some people do," Helen replied. We haven't progressed to that stage yet. We've only had the coach for a month."

Helen gave Rolf a mini-tour of the motorhome while Hank opened beers for himself and Rolf and a Sprite for Helen.

When they were settled in the lounge area of the Bounder Hank began: "Let's presume the hit-and-run wasn't an accident and that Griggs and Carter are complicit in the demise of Wengert. What would be the motive?"

"Well, if they did it, it most likely had something to do with the Soto shooting," Helen offered.

"OK, at the time of the hit-and-run, Wengert was not as yet identified as the shooter," Rolf said. "Maybe the motive would be to eliminate Wengert so he wouldn't spill the beans about whatever they have planned. If he would have been arrested as the shooter he would have been subjected to hard questioning by the FBI, with it being a hate crime."

"He was identified as the shooter, but he won't be spilling any beans in his condition," Hank said. "And we are the only ones trying to draw attention to the Battalion in this case. So far, it is a workable theory for a motive."

"It could be that Duesterbeck just didn't want to have the Battalion drawn into the investigation of the shooting," Helen added. "He figured that Wengert would eventually be caught. The media would quickly associate him with the Battalion and that would raise all kinds of speculation

43

about the Battalion being involved. And I'm sure the FBI would hound them."

"Now that Wengert has been identified as the shooter the Battalion can still be drawn into an investigation," Rolf replied. "However, with Engle keeping a lid on things the chance of the investigation being broadened is nil."

"If Wengert was indeed murdered there has to be a compelling reason, at least in their minds," Hank said. "Committing murder is an extreme step. We may be getting too far out in left field. If not, we need to discover the reason."

"What would happen if I stirred the pot a little by writing an additional news article? I would hint at the involvement of the Battalion in the Soto shooting," Rolf suggested. "The Battalion was involved in the Seymour rally the morning of the shooting and Wengert and his passenger most likely torched Wengert's truck to conceal evidence. I would also make sure the nearest FBI field office received a copy of the article."

"That might just work!" Helen replied. "An Indy field agent read one of Bill Anspach's columns and that's how an FBI agent was drawn into the investigation of the Leviticus killer last month."

"I would *love* to stir that pot a little," Rolf said. "It's always fun to find new ways to ingratiate myself with the local nutcases. I'll whip that up tonight and it will be in the morning edition. I better get moving if I want to make the deadline."

"OK, Rolf. It was a pleasure meeting you, and just maybe you can make something happen," Hank said. "I still have a gut feeling that there is more to be heard from the Battalion. I can't shake the idea that they have something planned."

"Well if they do, Hank, maybe my article will break something loose. I'll call you if I have anything of importance to report. Goodnight folks."

Chapter 5

Walter Duesterbeck trudged into the kitchen of the farmhouse and saw that the coffee had been brewed; his mother was up already. The morning sun was just peeking over the rise in the upper forty acre cornfield and started to illuminate the kitchen. He poured a cup and set it on the table to cool while he ventured out in his golf cart to the end of the quarter mile long, tree-lined drive to retrieve the morning paper.

He re-entered the house, sat at the kitchen table, took a sip of the tepid coffee, and scanned the front page of the paper. Noting nothing of interest, he turned to page two. The heading of an article caught his eye:

"Local group involved in Indiana shooting?"

His face reddened as he slowly read the story. The reporter rehashed the identification of Jason Wengert as the coldblooded murderer of Agusto Soto in the Indiana rest area over a week ago. The story then went on to mention the attendance of members of the Conservative Citizen's Battalion at the white power rally in Seymour, Indiana the morning of the shooting. Photographs of Jason Wengert and other members of the Battalion were included. It stated that the man with the handlebar mustache, Mr. Harry Griggs, was tentatively identified by a witness as the passenger in Wengert's truck when Wengert committed the shooting. *It is speculated*, the article said, *that the pair, in an attempt to destroy evidence, then set fire to the truck ninety miles north of the shooting on Interstate 69. Other members of the group most likely picked up Wengert and Griggs and drove them home to Michigan.*

The article concluded with questioning the hit-and-run death of Jason Wengert the following night. Sheriff Bobby Engle of Barry County maintained that the hit-and-run was a tragic accident, but others suggested that the death may not have been accidental.

Duesterbeck, upon finishing the story, quickly folded the paper and slammed it down on the kitchen table nearly knocking over his coffee cup. He arose from the table and grabbed the keys to his Escalade from the hook on the kitchen wall.

"Where are you going, Walter?" his mother asked. "I was just going to make you some breakfast."

"Don't bother,Mother. I have some things to do. I'll get something while I'm out."

And with that said he was out the door and speeding down the driveway.

Hank and Helen, upon reading Rolf's article, gave him a call.

"Hello, this is Rolf Kramden."

"Good morning, Rolf. Hank and Helen."

"Good morning, folks! You must have read the morning paper."

"That we did. The article was great. We hope it gets the intended results."

"We shall see, Hank. I emailed a copy of the story to the FBI field office in Detroit, although it's questionable if they will get involved. The Soto murder was solved and the Wengert hit-and-run is local."

"You're probably right about the FBI involvement. However, I would like to do a little more investigating, just to satisfy my own curiosity."

"What did you have in mind, Hank?"

"I would like to see the final coroner's report on Wengert and then take a look at the scene of the hit-and-run."

"You're in luck! I have a copy of the coroner's report, and I located the scene of the accident yesterday after I tailed Griggs to the Wal-Mart over in Hastings. The scene still had the police tape up at that point. They most likely removed it by now, but I am sure I can still find the site. I saved the coordinates in my GPS unit."

"Rolf, you're one heck of a reporter," Helen commented.

"Why thank you, Mrs. Moran. If you want, I can stop by with the coroner's report.My morning schedule would allow me to make a return trip to the scene of the hit-and-run. I can be there within the hour."

"We'll be waiting!" Hank said.

Rolf arrived at the campground forty-five minutes later and the three of them piled into his Prius. Hank sat in the front with Rolf, and Helen spread out in the roominess of the rear seat.

Rolf handed a copy of the coroner's report to Hank to read on the way, and they were off to Black Lake.

"I am going to take the scenic route over to Solomon Road," Rolf said. "We will be going right past the entrance to Duesterbeck's farm near Dowling."

Hank finished reading through the coroner's report and handed it to Helen in the backseat.

"What do you think of the report?" Rolf asked.

"Well," Hank replied. "Death was due to the penetration of the heart by a broken rib. Rib cage was broken in four places. Multiple bruises on the legs, but no broken leg bones and there were bruises to the facial area. Could have been a hit-and-run from a vehicle with a high front end, but the same damage could also have been inflicted with a piece of two-by-four."

"If he was hit by the phantom red truck you would think there would have also been some broken leg bones," Helen said. "It would have been difficult to break the larger leg bones with a two-by-four."

"Why are you thinking two-by-four instead of something like a tire iron as the weapon?" Rolf asked.

"A tire iron would have made distinct local bruises," Hank replied, "whereas with something like a two-by-four the damage would have been spread out, more like being hit with the grill and bumper of a truck."

"The one thing that bothered me was the location of the body after supposedly being hit head on by a truck," Rolf said. "One would think the body would have wound up directly on the road instead of fifteen feet off to the side in some tall grass."

"Perhaps the murderers didn't want to take the chance on being seen by passing motorists," Helen offered.

"That makes sense," Hank said. "I think we might be on the right track."

"I keep thinking that it would be awfully hard to smash a rib with the flat side of a two-by-four hard enough penetrate the heart," Rolf muttered as though thinking out loud. "The killing blow must have been made with some other weapon."

"I wish we would have taken a look at the chest area of Wengert's body when we had the chance," Hank said. "Coroner Holcomb asked how much of the body we wanted to look at and we said we only needed to see the face to make the ID."

"It might be worth a call to the coroner's office to ask a few questions about the injuries," Helen suggested.

"Let me pull over and we'll give Coroner Holcomb a call."

Rolf found a small highway department gravel storage yard a half mile farther down the road and pulled the Prius off to the side.

"I have the coroner's number on my cell directory. I have the phone synced to the Prius's audio system."

Rolf pushed a button on the steering column and told the phone to dial Coroner Holcomb. A few seconds later the coroner answered.

"Coroner, this is Rolf Kramden with the *Lansing State Journal*, and I have Mr. Hank Moran and Mrs. Helen Moran here with me. We would like to ask a few questions about the injuries to Jason Wengert."

"Yes, Mr. Kramden, I read your article in the morning paper and I found it quite interesting. And if I am on your speaker phone, how are you doing, Mr. Moran? I hope Mrs. Moran recovered from the ordeal of viewing Mr. Wengert."

"She's just fine, Coroner. She made a marvelous recovery."

"That's good to hear. Now, what would you people like to know?"

"Coroner Holcomb, you stated in your report that the cause of death was from a broken rib that penetrated the heart. Was there anything strange about the trauma of that particular area of the chest?

"I see where you are going with this, Mr. Moran. And yes, there was something a little strange with the discoloration of that particular area. There was a great deal of force applied locally to that area of the rib cage. My first impression was that he was hit by a hexagonal-shaped bar. But then I remembered that a lot of truck owners have deer or brush guards attached to the front ends. Most are factory made of round pipe to fit the particular model of truck, but I have seen some homemade ones that are actually made up of hexagonal steel bar weldments, which they then have chrome plated. They are quite strong and effective in minimizing damage in a collision with a deer. I estimated that the top bar of the guard would have been at the proper height to inflict the fatal injury."

"Coroner, I have a large wrecking bar at home in my garage that has that same hexagonal cross section," Hank said. "Is it possible that Wengert could have been struck with such an instrument?"

"Of course that is a possibility, Mr. Moran. But then how would you explain the rest of the injuries? They are all consistent with being hit by the front end of a vehicle."

"Coroner Holcomb, this is Helen Moran. You also stated in your report that there were no broken bones in Mr. Wengert's legs. Isn't that inconsistent with being hit by a fast-moving vehicle?"

"I agree, Mrs. Moran, that in most cases there are broken leg bones. But it is not out of the realm of possibility to have *no* broken leg bones. Wengert could have been leaping out of the way of the approaching vehicle when he was struck. Without his feet planted on the ground the damage to the leg area would have been less severe."

"Coroner, this is Rolf again. How do you account for Wengert's body being found fifteen off to the side of the road?"

"Well, Rolf, I have read reports of bodies becoming airborne when hit. The dynamics of such events depend on many factors. Fifteen feet is not an uncommon distance for a body to be thrown. As far as the direction to the side of the road, the best explanation is that he was leaping to the side when he was hit. His body could have been deflected farther to the side by the curved edge of a deer guard. I have seen some deer guards that are curved and that wrap around partially to the sides of the truck's front end. Without seeing an actual video of the event any explanation is pure conjecture. Like I said, there are many factors in the dynamics of such an event."

"Coroner Holcomb, I think those are all the questions we have for now," Hank said. "We thank you for taking the time to talk with us."

"It's been my pleasure, Mr. Moran. If you have any further inquiries please don't hesitate to call. I have made it a practice to keep an open mind in my line of business."

The call to Coroner Holcomb was ended and Rolf returned to the two-lane highway. When he pulled back onto the highway, he glanced in his rearview mirror and noticed a truck about a hundred yards back do the same. He had noticed the truck some distance back before they stopped to call the coroner. "I do believe we are being followed," Rolf said. "That blue pickup was behind us the whole way and it pulled off the road the same time as us."

"He's not being very secretive about the tail," Hank said. "Maybe the Battalion wants to make its presence known and try to scare us off."

"That could be. Harry Griggs drives a truck just like that one, but the driver is hanging too far back for me to make out if it's him."

Four miles farther down the road Rolf announced they were approaching the entrance to Duesterbeck's farm. He slowed and pulled over in front of the farm's entrance gate. The blue pickup that was following the trio pulled off to the side of the road a hundred yards to the rear.

There was an ornate wrought iron gate with curved brickwork on either side. An entrance code panel was mounted on a short pole on the left side of the entrance.

The house and farm buildings sat back off the road by two hundred yards. The driveway was paved and tree lined and the estate appeared to be well maintained. However, the target range was not visible, nor were the false front buildings for practicing urban warfare.

Rolf had seen the farm entrance numerous times. Hank and Helen, after having taken it all in, asked Rolf to continue to the site of the hit-and-run. The blue pickup once again pulled back onto the road in unison with Rolf's Prius.

They proceeded through the small town of Dowling, as well as Hastings—the seat of Barry County. On the Northwest side of Hastings, Rolf turned right onto Solomon road. Two miles up Solomon Road, Rolf slowed and turned onto a small dirt parking area, which was an access to the Middleville State Game Area. The blue pickup slowed but kept traveling north on Solomon road. Rolf was unable to ID the driver in his rearview mirror.

"Well, folks, we're here," Rolf said. "The actual site of the hit-and-run is about fifty yards to the north on Solomon. It's just a short walk."

The trio walked single file along the blacktopped road for the short distance to the site. "Here we go," Rolf said. "There is still a small piece of yellow police tape on that bush."

Hank stood viewing the site and then checked the blacktop in the immediate area. He said, "There are no signs at all on the road surface that a hit-and-run occurred. No traces of dried blood or tire marks. Let's see where the body was found."

The short path leading to where the body was found was well trampled. Fifteen feet from the edge of the road the grass still held an imprint of where the body had lain three days before. "Look, there are still traces of blood in the grass where his head was!" Helen said excitedly.

"What we need to do is check for any blood spatter on the nearby grass or bushes," Hank instructed. "Try not to trample any more grass than necessary. Just bend down and look very carefully in front of you as you inch along."

The three started off in different directions. A minute later Helen shouted, "I think I see some on this bush!" The bush was seven feet to the right of the body imprint.

Hank carefully maneuvered to where Helen was pointing. "Bingo! Do you know what this means?"

"I believe it means that Mr. Wengert was attacked here and not hit on the road," Helen answered.

Earlier that morning, Duesterbeck had sped out of his driveway and headed north to Hastings. On the way, he called Sheriff Engle to inform him he would be there in ten minutes for a meeting. He was visibly upset when he barged into Engle's office and forcefully swung the door closed.

"Christ, Walter! What has you in such a good mood this morning?" Engle said.

Duesterbeck had the morning *Journal* folded to the area of Rolf's article and slammed it down on the desk in front of Engle. "I gather you didn't read the morning paper, Sheriff. Take a look at the article that damn Kramden wrote and tell me where we go from here."

While the sheriff was reading the article Duesterbeck called Griggs. "Griggs, get your ass out of bed. I have something for you to do."

"I *am* out of bed, Major. What in hell do you want?"

"I need you to head into Lansing right away and tail that damned Kramden.

"You must have read the morning paper, Major. Somehow they found someone that identified me as the passenger riding with Wengert."

"That's why the hell I'm calling you. You need to stay on Kramden's tail this morning and see if he has any contact with that Moran guy. I think the way the article is written it is pure speculation, and they are just trying to stir things up."

"Looks like it worked. They sure got you stirred up this morning."

"Damned right it got me stirred up. You should be, too. Your ass is on the line if they come up with something."

"Don't you mean *our* ass, Major?"

When he ended the call to Griggs he turned back to Sheriff Engle, who had just finished reading the article. "Well, Sheriff, tell me how much shit we're in."

"What is this *we* shit, Walter? As far as my department is concerned, we conducted a proper investigation into the incident and came to a logical conclusion in accordance with the available evidence. I personally think you have nothing to worry about."

"Well, just remember this, Sheriff. If I go down for this, I guarantee you will, too. Now that *we* cleared the air, I am going back home to wait and see what Griggs turns up during his tail of Kramden today. I'll call if I need any of your *expert* assistance."

Griggs picked up Kramden's tail just as he was leaving home. He followed one-hundred yards behind the Prius, and fifteen minutes later, watched as Kramden drove into the Cottonwood campground.

Damn, he's heading right to the Morans', first thing! Griggs thought.

Griggs parked his pickup fifty yards past the campground entrance to await Kramden's next move. A short time later, the Prius exited the campground and headed west. He noted that there were now three occupants in the car. *Now where in hell would they be going so bright and early?* he thought.

Griggs followed the trio south on I-69, then west on State Road 79. Four miles later the Prius slowed and stopped at a highway department gravel pile lot. Griggs pulled off the road and viewed the trio with his pair of Nikon 8x40 binoculars. It appeared to him that they were just sitting there and talking.

After about ten minutes they were back on the road. Twenty miles later they approached Duesterbeck's farm and parked in the entrance. Griggs puller over a hundred yards back and called the major.

"Major, this is Griggs. Guess who is sitting out at your entrance gate."

"I'm in no mood for games, Griggs. For all I know, it could be fucking Santa Claus. Who is it?"

"I followed Kramden just like you said. He picked up the Morans at the campground, and now they're sitting right at your front gate."

"I see them on the security cam. It looks like they are just looking the place over. Wait! Now they are leaving. Just keep tailing them to see where they go."

"Major, I have a feeling they are heading to the spot where we took care of Wengert."

"Damn it,Griggs, never talk that openly when you call me. You never know who might be listening in." He sighed."You're probably right about their destination. I'm going to call Engle and have him dispatch a deputy to the site."

After finding the blood spatter at the site where Wengert was killed, Hank decided to have a further look around. "You two stay here. I'm going to go in a little deeper off the road to see what I can find."

"What are you going to look for, Hank?" Helen asked.

"A murder weapon," Hank replied.

While Hank was searching the area thirty to a hundred feet off the road, he heard the sound of a speeding auto go past the site. He thought he heard Rolf utter a few expletives. Fifty feet back from the side of the road he found a three to four foot length of lumber that was sticking nearly upright in a dense wild blueberry bush. The side of the two-by-six board that was facing him appeared to be stained with dried blood. The repose of the piece of lumber gave Hank the impression it was thrown in a high arc and was caught upright in the thick bush. Leaving the board untouched and in-situ, he made his way back the road.

As he approached Rolf and Helen, Hank could tell that Rolf was visibly upset. "What happened out here? I thought I heard an auto speed by, and then you giving someone the time of day."

"That S.O.B. nearly ran me down. We were just standing here, and Griggs swung all the way over to our side of the road doing about seventy. I could even see the bastard grinning ear to ear."

"Well, well, I guess it was Griggs tailing us all the way out here," Hank said. "Apparently he didn't like us snooping around the area."

"I got that impression," Rolf said. "But it just makes me wonder if these guys have any brains in their head at all. An act like that surely doesn't lower my suspicions. Anyways, Hank, did you find anything out in the boonies?"

"I sure did! A length of two-by-six treated lumber with blood stains. I left it right where I found it sticking up out of a blueberry bush."

Rolf gave Hank a strange look and said, "Earlier you speculated he could have been hit with a two-by-four. Now you found a two-by-six. That's pretty close. What's going on? How did you guess that?"

"It's fairly simple to explain. My old captain on the Kenner Police force could never understand it either. He said I was either psychic or practiced voodoo. Helen claims I'm just in tune to my intuitive feminine side. But it is simply the matter of boiling things down to the simplest possible answer. In this case the most readily available flat sided weapon would be a stout piece of lumber."

"Well, Mr. Sherlock Holmes, who are we going to report *this* to?" Helen asked with a chuckle. "We can't trust the sheriff's department. They would probably ignore it or destroy the evidence."

"Rolf, what jurisdiction do the state police have in Michigan?" Hank asked.

"The state police have the authority to conduct criminal investigations regardless of city, township, or county boundaries. I know what you're thinking, Hank, and I know someone who can help. I have a buddy at the headquarters in Lansing, and I am sure I can convince him to dispatch a trooper here within fifteen minutes. The trooper patrolling this district shouldn't be far away."

Rolf had a weak signal on his cell phone but was still able to contact his friend at the state police headquarters. After hearing Rolf explain the situation, his friend assured him he would have a trooper onsite in short order.

As the trio began walking the short distance back to the safety of the small parking area, a deputy sheriff's patrol car approached. They paused as the patrol car pulled to the side of the road and blocked their path. After a few short words on his radio, the deputy exited his patrol car and approached them. "Are you folks having any kind of trouble?" the deputy asked.

"No, we're not in any kind of trouble," Rolf replied. "Just out for a nice walk on a beautiful morning."

"I was told someone was out here messing around the scene of that hit-and-run accident. If you didn't already know, the scene is off limits due to an ongoing police investigation."

Rolf noted the deputy's name stitched into his shirt. "I am afraid you are behind the times a little bit, Deputy Seward. The crime scene tape has already been removed from the site."

"What is your name, sir?" Deputy Seward asked.

"I'm Rolf Kramden from the *Lansing State Journal*, and this is detective Hank Moran and his wife, Helen."

"Detective, huh. Just what is it you are detecting?"

"Oh, I am just helping out Mr. Kramden with his exposé article on the hit-and-run. And that is *retired* detective," Hank replied.

"Retired, huh? Well then you don't have any jurisdiction here do you?"

"No, none at all," Hank replied. "But that trooper approaching from down the road does."

They all watched as the state police patrol car slowed and pulled to the side of the road just past the deputy's patrol car and the group.

Deputy Seward recognized the trooper when he exited the car. "Hanratty, what are you doing here?"

"I was instructed to meet Mr. Kramden here to collect some additional evidence in the hit-and-run accident that occurred here last week."

"Hanratty, if there is any additional evidence to collect, the sheriff's department will handle it."

"I am afraid not, Deputy. Due to some alleged ineptitude on the part of the sheriff's department, the state police are now handling the case. Mr. Kramden, show me what you found."

Rolf introduced the Morans to Trooper Hanratty then led the way to where the body had lain. Rolf pointed out the bush with the dried blood to the trooper.

Hanratty noted where the body had lain relative to the distance to the bush. He photographed the scene, clipped the branches that contained the blood spatter, and deposited the clippings into a plastic evidence bag. "What else do you have to show me?" he asked.

"You'll have to follow me back off the road about forty more feet," Hank replied.

"Lead the way, Mr. Moran. Aren't you the retired detective who identified Wengert as the shooter in that incident at the Indiana rest area?"

"That was me, Trooper Hanratty. I found what could be one of the murder weapons back here stuck in a blueberry bush."

They found the bush with the two-by-six, and Hank pointed out the dried blood on the board. "I left the board exactly as I found it and I didn't touch it," Hank said.

"Good work, Mr. Moran. That sure looks like blood to me. Now all we have to do is find out if it belongs to Mr. Wengert."

Hanratty once again photographed the scene and, donning a pair of rubber gloves, extracted the board from the bush. The two then made their way back to the road to meet back up with Rolf and Helen.

Deputy Seward was waiting for them also. "What have you got there, Hanratty?"

"It's just a board Mr. Moran found back off the road a piece. If the blood on it turns out to be Mr. Wengert's, I am afraid we have a murder case on our hands,Deputy."

Deputy Seward, looking at first pale, then red faced, turned and headed back to his patrol car.

"I think he was a little upset," Rolf said.

Hanratty smiled and turned to Hank, "Mr. Moran, being an experienced detective, what do *you* think happened back there?"

"Well, Trooper Hanratty, my guess is that Wengert was murdered back there where his body was found. The actual murder weapon was most likely a large wrecking bar with a hexagonal cross section. He suffered a blow to the chest that fractured a rib, which then pierced his heart. The coroner found a chest bruise and imprint at the fractured rib that would match up with a hexagonal-shaped object such as a wrecking bar. The board was used to inflict the rest of the bodily damage to simulate being hit by an automobile."

"Well, we will surely consider that. OK, thanks for your input, Mr. Moran. I'll get this evidence back to Lansing and we'll take it from there. If indeed the blood does match up with Wengert's we'll let you know."

"Trooper Hanratty, Please keep *me* informed of your findings, too," Rolf said. "My readers will be anxiously awaiting the results."

"Will do, Mr. Kramden. And you people be careful now. Have a nice day."

As Rolf and the Morans walked past Deputy Seward's patrol car, they waved goodbye and noticed he was in a heated conversation on his cell phone.

When Deputy Seward returned to his patrol car he reluctantly made a call to Sheriff Engle. "Sheriff, Deputy Seward. That reporter, Kramden, and the Morans were just walking away from the scene when I arrived. I was talking with them when State Police Trooper Hanratty arrived. He said he was there to collect additional evidence on the hit-and-run. They found some dried blood spatter on a nearby bush and on a heavy board with blood on it."

"Seward, didn't you tell Hanratty that the sheriff's department was handling the case?"

"I did, Sheriff, but he said the state police were now handling it. He is going to take the evidence back to HQ to test the blood. He said if it turns out to be Wengert's blood, he thinks he has a case of murder."

"OK, Seward, you can head back here now."

"Will do, Sheriff."

Sheriff Engle sat back in his chair and pondered the latest events. Things appeared to be getting out of hand. He lifted the desk phone and dialed. Duesterbeck answered with an expectant tone. "What have you got, Engle?"

"You're not going to like this one bit, Major. It appears your boys really screwed up."

"What in hell are you talking about?"

"The state police are now involved. Kramden and the Morans found some evidence and reported it. I am afraid they now have jurisdiction on the Wengert case."

"What did those assholes find?"

"They found some blood spatter on a nearby bush and a blood spattered board that was located back off the road.

Your boys must have thrown the board away instead of taking it with them."

"I don't believe it! Those guys must have shit for brains! I thought they were smarter than that! Now what in hell do we do, Engle?"

"Nothing we can do, Major, but to wait for the proverbial shit to hit the fan."

Duesterbeck slammed the phone down. He opened his liquor cabinet and selected a 1.75 liter bottle of Old Grandad. He located a double shot glass in the overhead cabinet and with a shaking hand filled it with the bourbon. Without hesitation he emptied the glass and immediately refilled.

Chapter 6

It was mid-afternoon when Rolf dropped Hank and Helen off at their motorhome. "Guess what, Hank?" Helen said. "We were so wrapped up in our investigation we forgot that we were supposed to check out of the campground before noon."

"Time sure flies when you're having fun," Hank replied. "It looks like I better take a walk to the office. How many more days do you think we should extend our stay?"

"Well, we most likely won't hear any results on the blood test until tomorrow sometime, so I think we should allow for at least two more nights."

"That makes six nights total," Hank replied. "Why don't I just ask about the weekly rate? That will make it three more nights including tonight."

"Go for it!" Helen exclaimed. "But you know we aren't making much time on our tour. I hope we get out of the north country before we get stuck in the snow."

"We'll have to do some thinking about a plan B if we get waylaid here much longer," Hank suggested. "I can't believe it's nearing the end of August already. Maybe we should forget about the U.P. and Canada and head straight east to Pennsylvania after we are through here."

"OK, sounds like we have a plan B," Helen agreed. "Now we better get down to the office before we are booted out of here!"

Hank and Helen walked together down to the campground office. They told the clerk that due to some unforeseen circumstances they would have to extend their stay again for at least three more nights. The clerk checked the reservation book and said that she would have to do some juggling around on the incoming guests, but three more nightswouldbe acceptable. Helen asked about the weekly rate and the clerk replied, "If you stay six nights, the seventh night is free. So you would only owe for two more nights."

"Sounds like a deal we can't refuse," Hank replied.

With their reservation secured they walked back to the motorhome. It was only late August but Helen noticed there was a slight chill in the air. "I'm leaning more and more towards plan B," she said.

Back in the motorhome Hank couldn't stop thinking about Wengert's death. "Helen, I know we already concluded that Wengert had to be murdered if it turns out to be his blood on the bush and the board. And we also concluded that the only reasonable motive for the murder was to eliminate Wengert lest he screw up something that the Battalion has planned. Now all we have to do is figure out what their plans are."

"From what we've seen of the group so far, do you think they are smart enough to plan something that takes any brains?" Helen offered. "It wasn't very rational of Griggs to fake trying to run down Rolf and me with his truck."

"And it wasn't very rational for a murderer to toss one of the murder weapons just off the road, especially if they were trying to make it look like a hit-and-run accident," Hank added. "They should have taken it with them and burned it."

"Maybe we should dumb down our thinking as we try to figure out what they are up to," Helen said.

"Good point."

Late morning the next day, Hank called Rolf to see if there was an update on the blood tests. "Rolf, I know it's still a little early, but have you heard anything from Trooper Hanratty?"

"I talked to him about a half an hour ago. So far they have concluded that the blood is human and the types on both the bush and the board match Wengert's. DNA results won't be available until tomorrow morning. But here is the interesting part. He had blood type B negative, which is on the rare side. It is estimated that only one in sixty seven people have that type."

"That just about seals it for me!" Hank said. "What are the chances that someone with the same rare blood type would leave their blood behind in the same immediate area?"

"That was also Hanratty's conclusion, but he can't act on it until the DNA tests come in."

"Well, we'll be awaiting word on the DNA test results, Rolf. If nothing further arises we will be pulling out in two days. Why don't you stop over after work and we'll throw a few steaks on the barbecue grill."

"Gee, I'd like to, Hank, but I have a function I have to attend this evening as part of my reporting duties. One of our US senators is having a dinner cruise aboard the *Lansing Princess*. The senator is throwing a little party to thank his campaign staff and a few of his big donors."

"What's the senator's name?" Hank asked.

"His name is Kenton Westbrook," Rolf replied.

"Damn, Senator Westbrook. I forgot he was from Michigan."

"Sounds like you know him, Hank."

"I sure do. I guess you can say he once saved my life!"

Five Years Earlier

Detective Hank Moran and his partner, Detective Gerry Baker, had just arisen from their adjoining desks to follow some leads on the recent bank robbery in Kenner, Louisiana when Hank's phone rang. Hank tentatively decided to let it ring and quickly leave, anxious to pursue the bank robbery case. Then, thinking it might be another lead, he picked up the phone. "Detective Moran."

"Hank, you and Baker. Up to my office immediately," came the gruff voice of their boss, Captain Benson, Commander of the Investigative Services Bureau.

"Be right up, Captain."

"I heard him from over here, Hank. Right behind you," said Gerry.

Hank and Gerry paused in the doorway to Benson's office while Hank knocked on the doorjamb. Most of the day, Benson had a literal open door policy. The only times he closed the door was when he was partaking of his brown bagged lunch or when he was reaming someone out.

This time he told Hank to leave the door open and for him and Baker to have a seat. Hank and Gerry exchanged relieved glances as they sat, knowing they avoided catching hell today.

"Gentlemen, we are going to have a distinguished visitor arrive in the department within the hour. His name is Kenton Westbrook. He's a Yankee from Michigan. He is a US senator and carries a lot of weight in the reauthorization of the Community Oriented Policing Program, better known as COPS. As you know the COPS program helps us keep the officers we need out on the streets. Without it you two would be looking at early retirement."

"You want us to stand in the receiving line?" Gerry asked.

"No, smart ass. You and Moran are going to chauffeur the good senator around for two days. He asked to ride with the best detectives we have in order to get a first hand feel of what it's like out on the streets."

"What in the hell do we do with him in a dangerous situation?" Hank asked.

"Tell him to keep his ass in the car. We don't want CNN down here investigating the death of a revered member of the US Senate."

"Great! Can we cuff him if necessary?" Gerry asked. "I always wanted to put the manacles on a high ranking politician."

Benson just looked at him, showing the beginnings of a rare smile which he quickly managed to abort. "Gentlemen, be back here at eleven to hook up with the senator."

"Eleven, sir? What do we do with him for lunch?" Gerry asked.

"Take him wherever you want. Hank, you can put the senator's meal on your expense report. Just keep him out of Lucky's Lounge."

"Hell, you spoil all the fun, Captain," Gerry said.

"OK, we're through here. Be back at eleven sharp."

Hank and Gerry made a hasty exit out of the station and aimed their Crown Vic east on Veterans Memorial Boulevard. An informant named Squiggs said he had some late breaking information on the robbery of the Whitney Bank. Squiggs had been a reliable informant in the past so Hank's anxiety level had started to redline; he had a feeling this could be the break they were waiting for.

The FBI was already involved in the investigation and they were holding two New Orleans police officers in custody. Witnesses to the robbery said the robbers wore police uniforms and drove away in a New Orleans police cruiser. The FBI's lead investigator was a young agent named Chris Emory, who wanted to impress his superiors on his first big case.

Hank thought Emory was a little hasty in the arrest of the two officers, Parker and Fleming. The police cruiser could have easily been stolen in the continuing aftermath of hurricane Katrina. The NOPD, still in disarray, had not yet located all of their officers, let alone completed an inventory of all equipment and cruisers. Emory's arrest of the two officers seemed to be based on just the physical characteristics: the fact that they were the same heights and builds and had the same hair colors as the robbers. To complicate matters, they were seen in the area two hours before the robbery. The fact that they had unverifiable alibis did not help their situation.

Witnesses to the robbery stated that the robbers' uniforms seemed to be ill-fitting and they were wearing sneakers instead of the customary black oxfords. Hank strongly believed the uniforms had been stolen along with the police cruiser. His gut feeling told him the two officers were not guilty of the crime.

Hank and Gerry met up with Squiggs in the southwest corner of the Esplanade Mall parking lot. It so happened that Squiggs did have some very valuable information that was vital to the case. For the sum of two twenties Hank learned the location of the stolen NOPD patrol car. Squiggs said he saw it when he was walking back to his ancient Buick from one of his frequent quests for Mississippi River catfish. He claimed he had one on his line a few weeks ago that must have approached eighty pounds. He said a catfish that size would have fed him for a month. Hank urged him to continue with information pertaining to the case. Squiggs said he was walking past an abandoned factory at the foot of Duncan Street, which ended at the river, when he spotted the patrol car. It was partially hidden behind the building and would not have been readily visible due to the five foot high vine-covered fence around most of the property. Squiggs just happened to spot the rear end of the cruiser as he walked past a gap in the fence.

It was now rapidly approaching eleven a.m. and Hank and Gerry had to hurry to make it back to the station to meet with the senator. Gerry opened the window on his side of the Crown Vic and placed the bubble on the roof. Hank flipped on the siren and they were off. Five minutes later and two blocks from the station, Hank flipped off the siren and Gerry retrieved the bubble hoping the captain hadn't heard their speedy approach.

When they entered the station they were told to go right up to the captain's office. Hank was just about to knock on the doorjamb when Captain Benson looked up. "Ah, here they are, Senator, right on time."

Senator Westbrook rose from his chair and extended his hand. Hank and Gerry shook hands with the senator and noted his strong grip. Gerry thought he must have developed the grip on the campaign trail. He noted the smoothness of his hand and surmised that he surely didn't develop the grip from working for a living.

The senator seemed a couple of inches taller than Hank so Hank figured he must be about six two. He figured he must also work out because of no apparent gut or middle age spread.

After all the introductions were over Benson once again explained why the senator was in Kenner. The senator said he was anxious to get out on the street to gain firsthand experience in the daily life of a police detective.

"I'm glad you're anxious, Senator, because we have to get back out pronto. We just received a tip from a very reliable source on the location of the stolen police cruiser that was used in the robbery of the Whitney Bank."

"I hope you find it, Hank," Benson said. "This could just be the break we were hoping for. Senator, looks like you picked the right time to visit Kenner."

"Captain, could you arrange for a technician to be ready on a moment's notice?" Hank asked.

"Sure will, Hank. You'll have two at your disposal. And this time you have a legitimate excuse to use the siren."

Gerry shot Hank a look that said, *Damn, how did he know it was us?*

Hank just smiled and said, "Thank you, Captain."

They approached the old factory on Duncan Street and Hank slowed as they neared the gap in the surrounding chain link fence. There, just as Squiggs had told them, was the rear end of an NOPD patrol car sticking out from behind the building.

As they approached closer on foot they could see that the car had already been found by some opportunistic tire and wheel thieves. The car was sitting on its hubs with the engine hood open. Accessory parts on the engine had been stripped clean. Hank noticed the lack of rust on some of the machined surfaces of the engine block and knew the car was only recently abandoned.

"This has to be it!" Hank said. "It's a late model cruiser and was left here recently."

"It's bad luck the tire thieves got to it before you did," Westbrook said. "There's going to be fingerprints prints all over it."

"Well, Senator, maybe from the smorgasbord of prints we can also identify the car part thieves. We've been after them also," Gerry said.

Fifteen minutes after Hank's call to Captain Benson, two crime scene technicians were on the job dusting for prints. The battery was missing from the cruiser, so Hank was unable to pop the trunk lid. He was about ready to force it open when Westbrook said, "Why don't you use jumper cables and connect them to the battery cables and then to the battery in your cruiser?" One of the technicians said that wouldn't be necessary as they always carry a charged battery with them. As the tech went for the battery Hank thought, *This guy ain't so dumb.*

The tech touched the cables to the battery and Hank reached in with the end of a pencil and hit the button to pop the trunk lid. As he suspected, the spare tire was gone, but there, in the bottom of the trunk, lay the shirts and pants of two NOPD uniforms. After slipping on a pair of latex gloves he proceeded to go through the pockets of the uniforms. He was about to give up when he pulled a small scrap of paper out of the last shirt pocket. A phone number was hand written on the paper scrap.

"I've always had the feeling these guys weren't the brightest bulbs in the box," Hank said. He wrote the phone number in his small spiral notebook, then handed the scrap to the tech.

One hour later a wrecker appeared on the scene to transport the cruiser to the police department's garage for a more thorough inspection. However, the one piece of evidence Hank was anxious to work with was the phone number left in the shirt pocket. He was hoping it was placed there by one of the bank robbers and not by the patrolman who was the actual owner of the shirt.

"I assume you have a means of determining the owner of that phone number?" Westbrook asked.

"We sure do, Senator," Hank replied. "I'll call it in to the captain and the owner's name and address should be on my desk when we get back to the station."

The trio was back in the station in fifteen minutes. The captain's secretary, Marybeth, was just nearing Hank's desk as he approached. She handed him a large post-it note with the phone number written across the top. Under the number was the name Shirley Bashore and her address.

"What's next, Hank?" Senator Westbrook asked.

"I'm going to call the number to see if she is home. If she isn't home, we go and get a bite to eat." Hank dialed the number and let it ring ten times with no answer. "OK, let's go grab something to eat. It's now two thirty. If she works full-time she won't be home till at least four. I'll get one of our junior desk officers to check Bashore's S.S. records for a place of employment. We should have the information by the time we finish lunch."

Contrary to Captain Benson's orders Gerry persuaded Hank to head to Lucky's Lounge for lunch. Lucky, also known as Jack Boudreau, had an uncanny ability to pick more than his share of winning horses at the Fairgrounds Race Track every fall.

Gerry had a way of prying a few winning tips out of Lucky, but the reason they stopped there for lunch was because Gerry had told the senator that Lucky made about the best cheeseburger in Kenner and that the fries were second to none with Lucky's secret Cajun seasoned coating.

"This is a damned good cheeseburger," Westbrook said as he chomped through the half pounder. Why didn't Captain Benson want us to stop here?"

"Actually, he did want us to have lunch here. The captain knew if he told us not to, we would," Hank explained. "And on the rare occasion he doesn't brownbag he has lunch here, too."

Westbrook wonderingly wrinkled his brow, thought a second, then ate the rest of his fries.

As they were finishing their lunch, Hank's cell phone beeped indicating a message was received. "Ah, we have the lady's place of employment. It so happens she works as a secretary in a law office within walking distance of her apartment. She gets off work at four, and I have her driver's license photo to make an ID. Let's head over to her apartment and wait for her to come home."

At 3:45 the trio pulled into the lot and backed into a space with a view of the entrance to apartment 2C. Gerry explained to the senator that a detective will spend a lot of time sitting, waiting, and watching—that it is a learned skill.

At 4:15 Hank spotted Shirley Bashore approaching her apartment. "Let's give her about ten minutes to settle in then we'll go knock on her door."

At 4:25 Hank and Gerry exited the Crown Vic. Senator Westbrook opened the back door and started to get out also. "I'm sorry, Senator," Hank said. "You will have to remain in the car. Captain's orders. I am afraid this one we have to obey."

Senator Westbrook reluctantly returned to the backseat saying, "I assume you have orders to keep me out of harm's way."

"I'm sorry, Senator, but that's the way it is. The captain doesn't want you injured on his watch."

"You're just going to question a legal secretary. How much danger could that pose?"

"Ever hear of the term 'shit happens,' Senator?" Gerry asked, as he and Hank turned to walk to the apartment building. "Looks like the senator doesn't like taking orders," he said quietly to Hank as they approached the building.

They climbed the stairs to the second floor and found apartment 2C. Gerry knocked on the door and a few seconds later a female voice from inside asked who was there.

"Kenner Police, ma'am. We need to ask you a few questions," Hank said.

They then heard rapid footsteps. Footsteps from more than just one person. The apartment door opened but was stopped by the safety chain. There was a woman's scream, then a shot from a high caliber handgun as a hole in the door exploded outward in front of Gerry. Hank saw Gerry immediately go down. In an adrenalin rush Hank drew his 9mm as he kicked in the door and broke the chain.

He saw a man go out the front slider to the portico and go over the railing. He immediately followed.

Senator Westbrook heard the shot and was exiting the Crown Vic when he saw a man appear on the apartment's front portico. He saw the man start to lower himself from the railing with a gun in hand. As the man dropped the rest of the way to the parking lot, Westbrook saw Hank emerge from the apartment onto the portico. The man raised his gun and took aim on Hank who by then was at the railing. Westbrook shouted as he charged, and made a flying tackle, destroying the man's aim. The shot went wild as Westbrook and the shooter hit the ground. The shooter was driven face first onto the asphalt with a sickening crunch and he was immediately out.

Hank witnessed the Senator's flying tackle in disbelief.

"Are you OK, Senator?" Hank shouted.

"I'm fine, Hank," Westbrook replied.

"Well now that you got him, don't let him get up! I have to see about Gerry!"

Hank saw Shirley Bashore was pressing a towel over Gerry's chest wound and immediately called the station for an ambulance and backup. Hank checked Gerry's pulse and found it to be strong. At the same moment Gerry started to stir and opened his eyes. He made the motions of starting to get up off the floor.

"Hold it right there, partner. You are not getting up until the ambulance arrives," Hank commanded.

"What do I need an ambulance for? I just hit my head on the floor."

"Gerry, you hit your head on the floor because you fell backward when you were shot."

"I was shot? Am I alive? I didn't see any tunnel or bright light!"

"Gerry, you are very much alive, but you have a bullet wound in your chest."

"No shit? I thought something hurt a little bit."

Hank saw that Gerry's jacket was laying open and saw the exit hole of the bullet. He flipped his jacket over and saw the entrance point in the middle of the jacket's pocket. Reaching in the pocket, he pulled out Gerry's badge wallet. There was a bullet hole right through the center of the wallet. The corresponding hole in the badge was a perfect bulls-eye in the center circle which held the Kenner 'K'.

Hank showed the wallet to Gerry and flipped it open to reveal the badge. Gerry took one look at it and started to laugh. "I guess that's why they call it a shield. Oh hell, it hurts too much to laugh, Hank."

Hank knew he needed to get outside to check on Westbrook, but first he had to question Ms. Bashore. "Ms. Bashore, who was the man that was in your apartment?"

She answered rapidly, sounding panicky, "That was my cousin. He said he needed a place to stay for a few days. I have two bedrooms, so I said OK. I had no idea he had a gun. What did he do?"

"We're not totally sure yet, but we think he robbed a bank."

"Oh God, Donny Ray, What did you do?"

"OK, Ms. Bashore, keep pressure on my partner's wound. I have to check on your cousin's condition." Hank was more worried about the senator than Donny Ray.

When Hank ran down to check on Westbrook he saw he had retrieved Donny Ray's gun and was standing over the prone body. Hank immediately cuffed the unconscious shooter. "Where did you learn to tackle like that, Senator?" Hank asked.

"I had a very good linebacker coach at MSU back in the early eighties."

"Looks like you haven't slowed down much since, Senator."

"I try to keep in shape, Hank."

Just then wailing sirens announced the arrival of a patrol car followed by an ambulance. Hank directed the EMTs to the second floor to administer to Gerry and told the arriving officers to handle Donny Ray, telling them to call another ambulance if necessary.

"I guess Gerry was correct in what he told me fifteen minutes ago," Westbrook said.

"What was that Senator?"

"He told me 'shit happens.'"

"Yes it does, Senator. Yes it does."

Hank and the Senator followed the ambulance that was transporting Gerry to the hospital. They parked in a space near the emergency entrance and followed the gurney inside.

Gerry had been conscious for the fast trip to the hospital and waved at Hank and Westbrook as he was wheeled away to the ER.

The EMTs returned to the waiting room five minutes later and said the doctors were in the process of examining Gerry's wound. They told Hank that his partner was extremely lucky. They said the bullet struck Gerry's badge and case that he was carrying in his left jacket pocket.

Hank said that he had seen the badge and agreed that Gerry was indeed lucky.

One hour later Dr. Miller appeared from the ER. "I have some very good news for you gentlemen. Detective Baker is doing just fine. He is resting at the moment. We had to give him a sedative or else he would have been out here in person. He was an extremely lucky individual. Between penetrating the apartment door and his badge wallet, the slug lost enough energy so that it only entered his chest a short distance and lodged between two of his ribs. No vital organs were affected. We removed the bullet with no problems and sewed him up. He might have a few sore ribs for a week or two, but he should fully recover. He also suffered a slight concussion when he fell and struck the back of his head. Now, the scary part is that the entrance point of the bullet was directly over the left side of his heart. If he hadn't been carrying that badge in his jacket pocket I probably would have had some awfully grim news to tell you."

Westbrook said, "It's fortunate we went to Lucky's for lunch. It seems some of Lucky's good luck must have rubbed off on Gerry."

Senator Westbrook stayed only for the one day. He said he gathered more insight into the lives of a pair of police detectives in one day than he could have hoped for in a week. His wife, Clarice, undoubtedly had a major influence in cutting his tour short.

Westbrook told Hank to stop in for a visit if he ever got up Michigan way. They shook hands and Hank thanked the senator for tackling Donny Ray and destroying his aim, else he would be laying wounded in a hospital bed alongside his partner or worse.

Word of the senator's exploits spread rapidly and both the senator and Hank were interviewed by the entire local news media as well as CNN. For his brief stint in apprehending an armed bank robber Westbrook was immediately elevated to hero status. As for Hank and Gerry, they received a pat on the back from Captain Benson for a job well done.

After four hours of intensive questioning, Donny Ray Higgins confessed to the bank robbery. He gave up the name and address of his partner in crime, Charles Tucker, who was arrested the following day. The two NOPD police officers were fully exonerated.

Chapter 7

Present time

Having learned that Senator Westbrook was in the area, Hank was anxious to contact his old acquaintance. He checked the Internet and found that Westbrook had a regional office in Downtown Lansing. He punched in the phone number given on the site and his call was answered on the third ring. A soft female voice said, "Senator Westbrook's office. How can I help you?"

"This is Hank Moran from Kenner, Louisiana. Is the senator in?"

"I am afraid he is not here at the moment. He is out making final arrangements for a special events dinner this evening."

"I really would like to get in touch with him. Does he have a cell phone number that I can reach him at?"

"He has, but we don't give out his private number. Is there something I can help you with?"

"I met the senator five years ago down in Kenner, and he told me if I was ever in the area to pay him a visit. Would you please contact him and tell him Mr. and Mrs. Hank Moran are here in Lansing? I am sure he will want to talk to me."

"I will call him right away, Mr. Moran. Should I give him the number that is on my caller ID?"

The secretary read off the number and Hank told her it was correct.

Five minutes later Hank's phone rang. "Hank Moran."

"Detective Moran, I see you finally took me up on my invitation. How have you been?"

"I have been just fine, Senator. I officially retired last month and Mrs. Moran and I are doing some traveling. By the way, I hope you haven't had to make any more flying tackles in the last five years."

"No, Hank, I haven't. Clarice has strictly forbidden me to take part in any further police adventures. Say, how is Gerry Baker doing?"

"Gerry is doing just fine, as feisty as ever. He was back on the job two weeks after the shooting. He's got a new young female partner now and she is keeping him on his toes."

"I remember that day just like it was yesterday, Hank. It was uncanny how that bullet hit his badge wallet."

"The captain tried to give him a new badge, but he adamantly refused it. He insists on wearing his lucky badge with the bullet hole in it."

"Yeah, I can see how Gerry would be attached to it. Tell you what, Hank. I would really like to see you again. I am giving a dinner cruise this evening on the *Lansing Princess* riverboat. I would really appreciate it if you and your wife would attend. It will leave the dock at seven."

"I'm sorry, but we didn't pack any formal clothes for our trip, Senator."

"Don't worry about that, Hank. It's casual dress. You can come in shorts and t-shirt if you like."

"I think we can manage a little better than that, Senator. I am sure Helen would be delighted to attend."

"Great, I'll tell the staff to add you and Mrs. Moran to the boarding list."

"We'll see you then, Senator."

Helen emerged from back in the motorhome's bedroom as Hank was hanging up with the senator. "You'll never guess who I just talked with," Hank said with a smile.

"Let me see. Publishers Clearing House? We just won two million dollars," Helen answered.

"I'm afraid not," Hank replied. "But we were invited by US Senator Westbrook to a dinner cruise this evening aboard the *Lansing Princess*."

"The same senator who rode with you and Gerry for that day a few years ago?"

"The one and only."

"Holy cow, Hank. Did you accept the invitation? I don't have anything along to wear for a high-class dinner cruise."

"Don't worry about that. I told the senator the same thing but he said it's strictly a casual dress affair. He said we could show up in shorts and a t-shirt if we like."

"I can't imagine any affair put on by a US senator being casual."

"I can only go by what he said, Helen. It's just a small informal gathering to thank his local campaign staff and a few big donors."

"Well, in that case, I guess I can make myself presentable."

"Helen, you'd look presentable in the shorts and t-shirt."

"Yeah right, maybe twenty years ago. You know *you're* starting to sound like a politician now."

"Sweetheart, I could never hack it as a politician. You know I only report things strictly as I see them with no flip-flopping."

Helen retreated to the rear of the motorhome to check her wardrobe closet. She emerged ten minutes later. "OK, Hank, I have an outfit to wear this evening but no shoes to match. We need to go shopping!"

"Why? The senator said it's strictly casual. Can't you just wear your sneakers?"

Helen looked at Hank like a mother looks at one of her kids who just tracked mud across the kitchen floor.

Hank knew the look and said, "I'll get the keys."

Hank was just ready to start up the Honda when he uttered a "darn" and headed back into the Bounder. He came out a moment later with his recently acquired Kindle. He was a big fan of the 87th *Precinct* novels and was now prepared for the duration of Helen's quest for a new pair of shoes.

Helen directed Hank to the Eastwood Towne Center Mall and the Designer Shoe Warehouse. She had heard about the store from a fellow camper earlier that morning.

Hank sat outside the store reading while Helen shopped. A half hour later, Helen emerged from the store carrying a shopping bag and a big grin. "Now that wasn't so bad, was it?" she chided Hank.

"I'm amazed you found something so quick. I was prepared for at least a two hour stint."

"Actually, I eventually wound up buying the first pair I tried on," Helen excitedly explained. "I found a pair of brown leather open toed wedges for under fifty dollars."

Hank replied, "I'll be damned. May wonders never cease."

Two hours later back in the motorhome, Helen completed dressing and put the finishing touches on her makeup. She wore khaki colored capri pants with a brown tank top over which she wore a floral cardigan sweater. The ensemble was completed with her new pair of shoes. "Well dear, do I look *public* in this outfit?" she asked Hank as she approached him doing a fashion model's strut.

"Honey, you look more than public. Why don't we just spend a quiet evening at home," Hank said as he embraced her and nuzzled her ear. "After all, I see you have your T.C.B. bracelet on that I bought you at Graceland."

"Come on, big boy. We'll take care of business later. It's time to leave for the boat."

Hank slipped his sport coat on over his usual golf shirt and dress jeans and was ready. Helen glanced at him, raised an eyebrow, and said, "When we get back home, we're gonna have to take *you* shopping."

Duesterbeck's Farm - 6:00 PM

"OK men, I wanted to have one last meeting before we set out," Duesterbeck said. "If this doesn't turn out any better than Griggs' and Carter's debacle with Wengert, we are all going up the proverbial shit creek. Griggs, what in hell were you thinking when you threw the board away?"

"I didn't throw it, Major. When I saw Carter heave it, I immediately told him to go fetch it. But then we heard a car coming about a half mile down the road, so we jumped in my truck and took off. I didn't want my truck seen near the scene."

"I don't want to beat a dead horse, but we can't afford any mistakes like that tonight. Jacobs, I assume you are all set with the bartending job tonight?"

"No problem, Major. I put in a good word for you with the captain, and he said he could use you as I suggested. Hope you don't mind being paid minimum wage under the table."

Duesterbeck managed a chuckle, "Hell, all this fun and I get paid for it, too. Griggs and Carter, have you got your boats all set to do some fishing?"

"Yes sir, we'll be right behind you, Major."

"Just one more thing, make sure your radio batteries have a fresh charge. We have to remain in close contact. That's about it, men. You all know what to do. Let's do it."

The evening temperature along the river was pleasant with just a hint of the approaching fall in the air, typical in the northern climes in late August. Back in Kenner, Louisiana the air conditioning units would still be working overtime.

Hank and Helen were taking the now familiar walk from the Grand River Park parking lot down to the *Lansing Princess* riverboat when Hank took Helen's arm and stopped. "Doesn't that black Escalade look familiar to you?" he said to Helen.

"It sure does," Helen replied. "Same decals on the rear window and same tag number."

"Do you think Duesterbeck could be one of the senator's big donors?" Hank asked.

"He must be. I don't think a man like Duesterbeck would be on his campaign staff. The job would undoubtedly be beneath him."

"Well, there's only one way to find out. The boat is straight ahead."

There was a short wait on the gangplank as Captain Kerr once again greeted the arriving guests boarding the *Lansing Princess*. He was sure to mention to his incoming passengers that the handrail on the third and upper deck of the *Lansing Princess* was presently under repair. Not wishing to invite a possible tragedy on his cruise boat, Captain Kerr took the precaution of making the upper deck off limits to passengers until the handrail was adequately repaired. He had hired a guard to maintain a station at the top of the stairwell to turn back any roving guests that might venture that way. Kerr didn't want to take any chances for tonight's cruise, especially with the Senator's party on board.

Hank scanned the small crowd but couldn't spot Walter Duesterbeck.

Captain Kerr recognized the Morans as they approached his greeting station. "Welcome back. If my memory is correct, you are the good people from down in south Louisiana. Now let me think. Moran! Mr. and Mrs. Moran."

Hank could not believe the captain remembered their name and said as they shook hands, "You have an amazing memory, Captain. You are correct. Hank and Helen Moran."

"I am so glad you brought your lovely lady back to once again grace my vessel."

"Captain Kerr, I bet you flirt with all the ladies," Helen said as the captain lightly shook her hand.

"It's my duty to take full advantage of all the perks of being captain, Mrs. Moran."

"Well, I wouldn't want to prevent you from doing your duty, Captain. Your compliment is accepted."

As they walked towards the interior of the boat Helen said, "The captain is a charming gentleman."

"It was hard to distinguish who the politician is on board," Hank replied.

"Do I detect a slight bit of jealousy?"

"You're darned right. I don't appreciate other men coming on to you."

"Well, I think it's great that you still get a little jealous, Hank. I'll start to worry when you *quit* getting jealous."

"Well, sweetheart, you won't ever have to worry about having to worry."

"That sounded like a Yogi Berra quote. You're so dear," Helen said as she squeezed his hand.

"Your names, please?" asked a petite brunette with the name-tag Brittany.

"We are Hank and Helen Moran." replied Hank.

"Oh, so *you* are the Morans. Senator Westbrook requested that you be seated at his table. Follow me please."

Hank and Helen followed Brittany to a large round table on the starboard side located approximately midship. The table had place settings for ten and there were already three couples seated including Rolf Kramden and a female guest. Brittany stated that Senator Westbrook was delayed due to a late call to Washington but would be arriving shortly.

Rolf looked surprised to see the Morans onboard and doubly so for their seating at the senator's table. "Well, good evening, folks," Rolf said. "I remember you saying this morning that you were acquainted with the senator, but I didn't expect you to be here tonight."

"I am as surprised as you that we are seated at his table," Hank replied. "Are you one of the senator's big donors?"

"Heck no, Hank. I am the only member of the media on board and from what I hear the senator likes to keep the press under his thumb. Let me introduce you to the rest of these good people."

"On my right here is Rachael Harriman and her husband, Ted. Rachael is the senator's local campaign manager. On their right is Greg McAllister and his wife, Ginny. Greg is the senator's biggest fundraiser. And this lovely lady on my left is my fiancée, Linda Hartman. May I introduce Mr. Hank Moran and his wife, Helen, from Kenner, Louisiana. And, please, from now on everyone is on a first name basis."

"It's a pleasure to meet you all," Hank said.

"Have you lived in Louisiana long, Hank?" Greg asked. "I noticed you said 'you all' as two words instead of the southern y'all."

Hank chuckled and replied, "I've lived in Kenner and the New Orleans area all my life. There is a large segment of the area's population that has an accent that many people compare to New York City, mainly Brooklyn."

"That's very interesting," Ginny added. "What do you do down in Kenner?"

"I am a recently retired police detective."

"I remember now," Rachael exclaimed. "You are the detective that the senator met for the COPS legislation research about five years ago."

"That's right, Rachael. That was an adventuresome day for the senator. It was also an adventuresome day for my partner and me."

"If I remember correctly your partner was actually shot. Did you ever realize that that one day provided the inspiration for the legislation's renewal? Senator Westbrook even tried to have the legislation named after your injured partner, but other members of the senate protested saying there were hundreds of other injured police officers across the country that would be just as deserving."

"Ahh, I see you have all met," said Senator Westbrook as he and his wife approached the table. Hank and Mrs. Moran, I am really glad you could make it this evening."

The group rose from their chairs to acknowledge the senator's arrival.

"We wouldn't miss it," Helen replied. "And, please, call me Helen."

"Helen, I am Clarice, Kenton's wife. I never got a chance to meet you when we were down in Kenner."

"It's a pleasure to make your acquaintance," Helen said as they lightly shook hands.

There was a slight tremor as the *Princess* moved away from the dock to begin the cruise.

"Everyone, please be seated," the senator commanded. He remained standing and tapped his water glass with his dinner knife to get the attention of all the guests. He then proceeded to give a short welcome address and thanked everyone involved for their support in his continuing bid to hold on to his senate seat. Afterward a short prayer was offered by the reverend of the senator's local Episcopal Church.

With all the formalities over, Westbrook summoned the table's private waiter with a wave of his hand. Captain Kerr had made all the preparations necessary to make sure the needs of a distinguished guest like the senator would be met with the utmost service.

"Good evening, ladies and gentlemen. My name is Jordan and I'll be your server this evening. The captain extends his greeting with a few bottles of his choice chardonnay and merlot wines. You have a choice of two entrees this evening," Jordan proceeded to explain. "Chicken cordon bleu with creamy white wine sauce or filet mignon over lobster Boursin mashed potatoes with merlot sauce. Now as for the wine may I suggest the chardonnay for those ordering the chicken cordon bleu and merlot for those partaking of the filet mignon?"

Jordan proceeded to open and pour the desired wines. "May I assume your choice of wines indicates your choice of entrees?"

"You may assume that on my behalf," Senator Westbrook said.

With no exceptions the rest of the party agreed that Jordan's assumption was correct. After noting how those who ordered steaks wanted them prepared Jordan replied, "Excellent. Salad will be served shortly."

When Jordan left Westbrook said, "So, Rolf, are there any breaking stories we may get the skinny on?"

"Actually, Senator, I am working on something that involves Hank and Helen."

"If Hank is involved it must be some kind of an investigation into a criminal matter," the senator said smiling.

"Actually you're right, Senator," Hank replied. "We happened upon something on the drive up from Louisiana and it seemed to follow us right here to Lansing."

"Are you going to keep us all in suspense, Hank? You have our undivided attention."

"Well, Rolf is working on the story, so I'll let him tell it. I don't know how much he wants to reveal at this point."

Rolf went on to give a brief synopsis of the murder of Agusto Soto in the Indiana rest area and how it related to the hit-and-run death of Jason Wengert over in Barry County. He also made mention of the additional evidence found at the hit-and-run scene and the possible involvement of a white supremacist group headed by Walter Duesterbeck.

When Rolf's presentation was finished Hank said, "Rolf, I noticed Duesterbeck's SUV in the parking lot when we arrived. I assumed he would be on board the boat but I haven't spotted him yet."

"That's interesting," Rolf replied. "A member of the CCB is tending bar at the rear of the boat. His name is Stan Jacobs. He also attended the rally down in Indiana. I do know that tending bar for special events on the *Princess* is one of his regular gigs."

"You sure keep tabs on these guys, don't you? Does Duesterbeck ever work on the boat?"

"Not that I'm aware of. I do think he would consider it too menial."

"Senator, is Walter Duesterbeck on your list of invitees?" Hank asked.

"I prepared the invitations and there is no one by the name of Duesterbeck on the list," Rachael answered for the senator.

"Hmm, well I doubt that he is providing valet service out in the parking lot. I wonder if he just happened to drop Jacobs off," Hank pondered.

"I don't think so," Rolf answered. "I happened to walk past Jacobs' Dodge Ram when I arrived."

"Maybe I should spend more time at home in Michigan instead of DC," Westbrook said. "I seem to be out of touch when it comes to all the militias in this fair state of mine."

"Well, Senator, if you need to be filled in on the topic Rolf is the man to talk to," Hank added. "He keeps close watch on all the groups."

"I really do need to learn more about all the radical groups in the state. After all, I am co-sponsoring a bill that would add further restrictions to the ownership of assault weapons."

"Senator, I think you will become extremely unpopular in Michigan when word gets around that you are fostering such a bill," Rolf added. "Half the male voting population either belongs to the NRA or relates to their philosophy."

"Well, Rolf, that's the chance I'll have to take. I am also afraid the word about my bill is already out. My staff has received calls from some disgruntled citizens complaining about it. But some sanity needs to be restored with regards to the issue. Our police are rapidly being outgunned. I have come to realize that the situation with yahoos running around with assault weapons has no place in a civilized society."

Everyone at the table wholeheartedly agreed with the senator. Especially Hank, who had gleaned firsthand knowledge during his thirty two year law enforcement career.

"Well, enough of that sobering talk," Westbrook said. "I see Jordan making his way toward us with a cart full of goodies."

Jordan deftly distributed the cart full of salads and fresh baked rolls. After refilling the wine glasses as needed he said, "Enjoy your salads, everyone. The entrees will be ready in a jiffy."

"Helen, I noticed your bracelet when we shook hands," Clarice said. "What does T.C.B. stand for?"

"It stands for taking care of business," Helen replied. "Hank bought me the bracelet in the Graceland gift shop. 'Taking Care of Business' was Elvis's favorite motto."

"Helen is sure that Elvis is still taking care of business at Graceland," Hank said. "She claimed she saw his ghost while we were touring the mansion."

"I'm sure Hank never believed me, but the tour guide said his ghost was seen on many occasions."

"Ooh, tell us about it," Ginny excitedly said. "I read about the sightings in Graceland but never talked with anyone who actually saw him."

"Well, I was at the rear of the tour group with my back to the hallway when I felt a chill on the back of my neck. When I turned around I caught a glimpse of a dark haired man in a white jumpsuit pass the doorway and head up the stairs. I told the tour guide that I thought it was great that they had an Elvis impersonator to follow the group. She said they had no such thing. That's when she told us about the many other sightings. Later, when we crossed the hall into the next room, I saw a man in a white painter's jumpsuit working at the top of the stairs. At first I thought I was mistaken about seeing Elvis, thinking I saw the painter. Then I remembered that the jumpsuit I saw had fringes and jewels on it. The painter had on a plain white suit."

Hank thought, *Well darn, maybe she actually did see his ghost*, then said, "Hmm, I saw the painter working at the top of the stairs and thought you were mistaken. You never told me about seeing the fringes. I should know better than to doubt your observational skills."

"You didn't fool me, Hank Moran. I knew that's why you had that silly grin on your face for the rest of the tour."

"Well, I'll be.You noticed that, too?"

"Just be careful, big boy, you have no idea of the things I notice."

Laughter erupted from the rest of the group at the table on Helen's last remark and upon seeing Hank's reddening face.

"Well, I think you just took care of that business, Helen," Clarice added prompting more laughter.

Ten minutes later Jordan and two assistant waiters appeared with trays full of the entrees. Both the chicken cordon bleu and the beef filet dinners looked so delicious to Helen that she decided she wanted to share meals. After a mild protest from Hank he cut his filet in half and accepted half of Helen's chicken. Hank thought he was getting the bad end of the deal until he tasted the chicken, which titillated his taste buds into a mild state of euphoria. Helen tasted the chicken also and wanted the portion she had given to Hank back, but Hank said no way, a deal was a deal. Just to play it safe Hank rotated his plate so that the chicken was on the far side away from Helen just in case she had intentions of pulling a heist with her dinner fork.

Helen watched Hank rotate his plate and then looked at him and said, "Smart ass."

The other diners at the table were watching the exchange between the Morans with amusement and burst out in laughter at Helen's rebuke.

With the dinner winding down and coffee and raspberry cheesecake being served, a jazz trio began playing their rendition of Miles Davis', "Blue in Green."

"Well," Senator Westbrook said as he arose from the table. "If you good people would excuse me, I need to make my rounds of all my other guests. Please enjoy the rest of the evening and the trio's dance music."

Chapter 8

The message went out on the TriSquare radio, "This is the major. All units report in."

The three replies came in the predetermined order.

"Interceptor One in position, sir."

"Interceptor Two in position."

"BT waiting for instructions."

"Be alert. Future comms in text mode."

Captain Kerr took note of the two small outboards as he piloted the *Princess* upriver. It was not uncommon to encounter night fishermen on the river during his evening cruises. The one outboard slipped behind the *Princess* and motored out of sight. The second small boat maintained a steady one hundred yard distance ahead of the *Princess*. *Probably trolling,* the Captain thought. *I'll have to be more vigilant as darkness approaches.*

Senator Westbrook spent the next hour hobnobbing with his guests. Drinks were flowing freely aboard the boat, and the guests made use of the dance floor as the trio picked up the beat.

Clarice Westbrook kept a watchful eye on her husband. "Kenton, I think you should slow down on the spirits. You know we have to catch an early morning flight back to D.C."

"Yes Clari, I know you are right, but these people deserve my attention after all their hard work on my behalf."

"I know everyone desires your attention, but you can assuage them just as well without a drink in your hand."

"Once again I will accede to your better judgment, Clari," the Senator replied as he handed his wife his drink.

Clarice noted the strong odor of alcohol wafting from the glass. "Kenton, this smells like straight scotch."

"Well, I asked the bartender for scotch and water, but he said he had a bottle of twelve year old Macallan single malt that would be a shame to dilute with water. I wholeheartedly agreed, so he has been pouring double shots over ice for me."

"Good lord, I'm glad I caught you when I did. Now, please, stay away from the bar."

"Clarice, your wish is my command," the senator replied with a wave of his hand and a bow.

Jacobs felt the vibration in his pocket and paused from his bartending duties to read the text message on his radio.

"Old girl nearing turn. All units on alert. BT, how is dolphin progressing?"

"Intake as planned," Jacobs replied.

"Keep pumping, BT."

Hank and Helen spent most of the last hour on the dance floor. Helen couldn't remember the last time Hank enjoyed himself so much. She thought he was finally learning to relax without having to think about the murder or robbery cases that always occupied his mind as a Kenner detective.

"It looks like retired life is starting to agree with you," Helen said as they left the dance floor to sit the next one out.

"I think it is," Hank agreed. "I forgot what a good dancer you are. I should have taken you out more often."

"Well, big boy, you have the rest of your life to make up for it. And, you better keep yourself in shape if you intend to keep up with me."

"I haven't been doing so bad so far, have I?"

"You're doin just fine, dahlin," Helen replied in an exaggerated southern drawl as she squeezed Hank's hand.

"It is getting a little warm in here though. Let's venture up to one of the upper decks and get some fresh air," Hank suggested.

Rolf and his fiancée were seated at the table and heard Hank's remark. "I understand the upper deck is off limits tonight," Rolf offered. "It seems a portion of the handrail is under repair."

"That's OK, the second level has a promenade," Hank replied. "We explored the boat the other day when we took the luncheon cruise and I reported the loose handrail to the captain."

"Well then, you two go ahead. Linda wants to try to wear me out on the dance floor," Rolf replied.

Hank and Helen made their way to the stairwell near the stern of the boat. They noticed the large hand printed sign stating that the third level was closed due to repairs. The sign was sitting on an easel in the corner of the first landing. They reached the second level and entered the starboard side promenade. The *Princess* was slowing as it approached the turnaround point of the cruise.

Hank enjoyed watching the boat maneuver its change in direction. The river wasn't wide enough to make a normal U-turn so with the aid of the thrusters the boat seemed to pivot as on a turntable.

"Boy, that was a smooth maneuver," Hank said. "I'll bet the folks down on the dance floor hardly noticed."

"With the amount of alcohol they're consuming I don't think they could tell one way or another if their swaying was due to the boat or the drinks," Helen replied.

"I am sure a lot of aspirin will be consumed in the morning."

"I'm glad we took a little breather when we did," Helen said. "I do believe I was getting a little tipsy myself. I think the senator was, too. Clarice told me she cut off his drinks because they have an early flight back to D.C."

"Yeah, I noticed he wasn't feeling any pain before we started our little stroll," Hank replied.

Jacobs once again felt the vibration in his pocket and read the single line message on the radio's screen.

"Send the dolphin. ASAP."

Jacobs saw the senator about fifteen feet from the bar and called to him. "Hey, Senator, can I talk with you a second?"

Westbrook raised his finger to signal Jacobs was heard and for him to wait a second. When the senator finished making his point with one of his guests, he made his way to the bar. "No more drinks, barkeep. My lady cut me off."

"That's OK, Senator. The reason I called you over is that I just got a message from Captain Kerr. He said he needs to talk with you up in the wheelhouse."

"Oh? OK, point the way, barkeep."

"The stairwell is over there to your left. At the top of the stairs hang a right. The captain is waiting."

"Thank you, good sir," Westbrook replied and unsteadily made his way to the stairs.

Jacobs waited until the senator was out of earshot and reported in on his radio, "Dolphin on his way."

He then motioned to his fellow bartender to take over. "I need to take a break, Jim. Can you handle the bar for a while?"

"Sure thing, Stan, you've been hogging all the tips anyway."

"Jim, you'll get more tips if you improve your bar-side manner. Remember. Service with a smile!"

Jim gave him the finger along with a big smile and said, "Service this."

Jacobs turned away laughing and made his way to the stairs, staying well behind the senator.

Senator Westbrook reached the top of the landing on the upper deck and paused to get his bearings. He was momentarily confused as to which direction led to the front of the boat and the wheelhouse. Then a man's voice beckoned to him, "Senator Westbrook, can I have a word with you please?"

Westbrook turned and squinted into the dark aft end of the boat, "Captain Kerr? I thought the wheelhouse was in the other direction."

"It is, Senator. And I'm not the captain."

"Well, who are you? And what do you want?"

"I am Major Walter Duesterbeck from the CCB, better known as the Conservative Citizens Battalion. The Battalion has a slight problem with the new anti-gun legislation you are trying to push through Congress."

"Duesterbeck, huh? I heard about you and your group of misfits earlier this evening. It seems you and your so-called battalion will soon be under investigation for the murder of one of your colleagues."

Duesterbeck was momentarily taken-aback at the senator's statement. "Who told you such a preposterous thing?"

Before the senator could answer Jacobs appeared from behind. "Major, that news reporter and detective that have been snooping around are onboard. In fact, they were seated at the senator's table."

"Well, it seems like the Morans have a penchant for riverboat cruises. We might have to invite them to our little party. Anyhow, Mr. Senator, let's get back to the point in question. The CCB, on behalf of the majority of law abiding citizens in the state of Michigan, request that you drop the well-intentioned but misguided legislation you are authoring."

"Mr. Duesterbeck, in all good conscience, I have to deny your request. The legislation I am proposing will only tighten up the licensing process to make it harder for *criminals* to obtain automatic weapons. Law abiding citizens should have no problem with it."

"That's where you are wrong, Senator." Duesterbeck replied. "We know that each small piece of new anti-gun legislation is part of the overall plan to eventually deny all citizens the right to bear arms. The right to bear arms is guaranteed by the Constitution and we will fight anyone who attempts to deny us that right."

"I think you people are a bit paranoid. I will be returning to Washington tomorrow and the legislation will be introduced the next day. Now goodnight, gentlemen."

Anger rapidly built in Duesterbeck and he nodded to Jacobs who was still standing behind the senator. Westbrook turned to leave and was immediately struck on the side of the head with the now half empty bottle of Macallan twelve year old single malt scotch.

When Westbrook hit the deck, Jacobs uncorked the bottle and poured a generous amount on the unconscious senator. It wasn't difficult for the two battalion members to slide the senator's limp body through the unrepaired opening in the boat's handrail. Jacobs replaced the cork in the scotch bottle and tossed it overboard, hoping it would float near the senator in the Grand River nearly thirty feet below.

Duesterbeck immediately switched on his radio and announced, "Dolphin in water."

One deck below, Helen heard what she thought were some men conversing on the deck immediately above their position.

"Hank, there are some men talking just above us."

"It's probably Captain Kerr instructing one of his crew members."

"I don't think so. The wheelhouse is up near the bow. I think I heard someone say our name."

A short while later the conversation seemed to get louder but still unintelligible over the drone of the *Princess*'s diesel engines. "I may be mistaken," Helen said, "but I think I heard the senator talking up there."

"Well, he was making his rounds like the expert politician that he is. He might be talking up his virtues to some of the crew members."

The words were no sooner out of Hank's mouth when a body came plummeting down four feet in front of them and splashed into the river seventeen feet below.

"Holy shit," Hank said. "I'm sure that was the senator. Throw me one of those preservers."

Hank quickly slipped off his shoes and jacket, emptied his pockets, and vaulted the promenade's banister. He made a splashed entry into the river feet first. Helen found the life preservers and in a frenzy tossed three of them overboard, hoping one of them landed near her husband. "I have to alert the captain," she shouted, as she bounded up the stairs to the upper deck.

Upon reaching the third level she immediately came face to face with a man she recognized as the bartender from the senator's party. She was grabbed by the arm and forced further to the stern. "Let me go!" Helen hollered. "I have to get to the captain! There are men overboard!"

"I am afraid our captain will learn of no such thing, Mrs. Moran," said a voice she quickly recognized. "Hang on to her, Jacobs. We'll have to take her with us."

"I'm not going anywhere with you, Duesterbeck," Helen said as she struggled to free herself. Despite a few good, well-placed kicks she was expertly subdued as a large hand was clamped over her mouth and she was forced to the deck.

"Hold her there while I get the tape." Duesterbeck said as he located his small duffel bag. He had brought the bag along, which contained an assortment of items he deemed might come in handyin case their plans didn't come off as expected.

He found the small bottle of chloroform and poured a generous amount onto a hand towel. Jacobs removed his hand from Helen's mouth, but she had no time to shout out as the hand was quickly replaced by the chloroform-drenched towel. Duesterbeck held the towel in place over Helen's nose and mouth until he felt her body go limp.

"Here's the duct tape, Jacobs.Wrap her up good while I signal for Carter."

"Interceptor Two. Pickup ASAP!"

Captain Kerr saw the small outboard appear off the port-side bow and seem to pass by the *Princess*. He paid the small boat no further attention as he would rather have the fisherman towards his rear instead of in his way. He sensed what he thought was a small disturbance at the aft end, but figured it was just the guard he had hired doing his duty in keeping inebriated guests off the third deck.

Chapter 9

The Grand River was in a serene mood. The surface was rapidly becoming sleek and smooth as glass after the passing wake of the *Lansing Princess*.

Hank had surfaced and was treading water when he spotted one of the life preservers in the rapidly fading reflection of the boat's party lights. He swam the fifteen foot distance and slipped the strap of the preserver over his shoulder. The river water was cold but bearable and he had no immediate fear of hypothermia. He paused to listen.

He could hear some faint splashing, which he estimated was thirty yards upstream from his position. He hoped it was the senator. Despite the combination of the current flowing in his direction and his swimming upstream he hoped he would reach the senator in time.

In what seemed like an eternity but was only about two minutes his left hand landed upon a rapidly thrashing arm. "Senator! Calm down! I have you!" Hank shouted. "You're going to drown us both."

In his frenzy the senator grabbed Hank with both arms and forced his head under water. Hank was able to keep a hand on the preserver and resurface. He grabbed one of the senator's hands and forced it to the preserver. "Senator! Hang on to the preserver," Hank shouted again.

The senator's hand finding purchase on the preserver had an immediate calming effect. "OK, Senator, just hang on to the preserver and keep treading water," Hank said. "I'll try to make it to the bank."

The senator was rapidly gaining his senses and managed to weakly speak, "Hank, is that you?"

"The one and only, Senator. Just keep treading. Life has its ups and downs. The trick now is to stay up."

"We're in the middle of a river hanging onto a life preserver and you're waxing philosophical."

"Good a time as any, Senator. Just hang on. I take it you don't know how to swim.

"Unfortunately, swimming is not one of my many talents," the struggling senator said.

"OK, I'll try to make it to the north bank with you in tow." Facing downstream Hank knew the north bank was to his left, the same side of the river as the *Princess*'s dock.

Carter did a tight U-turn as the *Princess* floated past and nudged the fourteen foot outboard up to the riverboat's rear rescue platform. Duesterbeck secured the line and steadied the small craft. Jacobs, carrying Helen's limp body over his shoulder managed to lower himself to his knees. "Carter, grab her feet, she's going with you."

Carter grabbed Helen by the ankles and backed up far enough in the boat to place her legs over the boat's second seat. He then moved forward, and with him and Jacobs each grabbing an upper arm, managed to place Helen in the boat with her rear on the floor and her head resting on a floatation cushion. Carter then swung Helen's feet and legs forward so that she was lying on her side in a curled up fetal position in the bottom of the boat. "Sleep tight, lady," he said.

"Carter, go to the boat ramp and leave her in the boat when you trailer it, then cover her up with the tarp," Duesterbeck said. "She shouldn't come to until you get to the farm, but just in case, take this bottle of chloroform and the rag with you. If need be, give her another whiff. Jacobs and I will get back to work like nothing happened." Duesterbeck untied the outboard from the *Princess* and Carter shifted the fifteen horsepower Mercury motor into reverse. After safely backing away from the *Princess* he shifted into forward and veered away.

When Jacobs turned away to return to his bar-keeping duties he heard the major radio to Griggs. "Interceptor Two. Two dolphins in water. Repeat two dolphins."

After receiving the major's message Griggs slowly motored the boat downstream shining his high candle power LED flashlight in sweeping arcs across the smooth surface of the river. He could see the fading lights of the *Princess* as it continued on its journey a half mile downstream. Knowing his quarry should be in his immediate vicinity he slowed the boat and more slowly arced the light across the river's glassy surface.

His light finally found the pair hanging onto a life preserver with one of them trying to swim one-armed to the bank.

The *Lansing Princess* slowed as Captain Kerr started the boat's docking maneuvers. Knowing the evening cruise was drawing to an end, Clarice Westbrook started the search for her wayward husband. She made her way through the guests inquiring about the senator, but most said they hadn't seen him for the last half hour or more.

She arrived at the aft end bar just as the bartenders declared the bar was closed. "Have either of you gentlemen seen my husband?" she asked them.

"The last I saw the senator he was heading toward the stairwell. That was over a half an hour ago," Jacobs answered. "Maybe he went up to chat with the captain."

On her way to the stairwell Clarice stopped at her table to pick up her purse. Rolf and his fiancée were gathering their things and making preparations to leave. "Any luck finding the senator?" Rolf asked.

"Not yet," Clarice answered. "The bartender said he saw him heading to the stairs a while ago."

"The Morans went up to the second deck to get some air. Maybe he's up there reliving old times with Hank," Rolf said. "Come on, we'll head up there with you. I want to say goodnight to the Morans before we head home."

As they were approaching the stairs a tall man turned from the landing and headed towards the now lowered gangplank. Rolf paused to try to identify the man, but with his back turned towards him in the dim light he couldn't make out who it was.

They could not find the Morans or the senator when they reached the second deck promenade. Rolf was about to turn to head up to the upper deck when he spotted what appeared to be a small pile of clothing on the aft end deck of the promenade. "Wait here a second," he told the two women. "I want to see what that is on the floor."

As Rolf approached the pile he could see it was a jacket and a pair of shoes. A wallet and a set of keys were stuck in one of the shoes. He picked them up and returned to Linda and Mrs. Westbrook. "If I'm not mistaken, this is the jacket Hank was wearing."

"You're right," Linda said. "What would his jacket be doing there with his shoes?"

"I have a bad feeling about this," Clarice said.

Helen was conscious the whole time the three men were placing her in the boat. She had managed to hold her breath when she smelled the chloroform laced rag that was held over her face. She decided to play possum and pretend to pass out before she ran out of breath. It was a close call, but Duesterbeck removed the rag just in time. The minimal dose she received of the old fashioned anesthetic had only a slight lightheadedness effect.

She didn't dare move as the driver of the boat kept a close watch on her while he headed to the boat ramp which was a half mile upriver from the *Princess*'s dock. Helen saw the lights of the *Princess* pass her position as the boat she was in steered into the ramp area. She saw the man leave the boat and peered over the edge as he walked away. A few minutes later a boat trailer and taillights from a pickup truck appeared. She quickly lowered her head and once again tried to appear unconscious. She didn't want to risk another dose of chloroform.

She felt the boat move and heard a metallic clink as the winch line was attached to the bow eye. She then felt the boat rise up and settle onto its trailer. Helen managed a quick peek over the edge of the gunwale as the truck pulled the boat and trailer from the water. It appeared no one else was at the boat ramp area.

When the rig came to a stop she quickly laid down again. Helen smiled, as she had heard the man's instructions by Duesterbeck and she knew the boat was about to be covered with a tarp.

Captain Kerr was just exiting the wheelhouse as Rolf and the two women approached. "Captain Kerr, have you seen my husband, the senator?" Clarice asked in near panic.

"Mrs. Westbrook, I saw the senator when he boarded the *Princess*, but I haven't seen him since. Why? Is something wrong?"

"He is missing! We looked all over the boat and can't find him!"

"We found this jacket, wallet, and pair of shoes on the second deck promenade," Rolf added. "They belong to Hank Moran. We can't find him or Mrs. Moran either."

"There must be a simple explanation," the captain answered. "Are you sure they didn't leave the boat after we docked just now?"

"Captain, I am sure my husband wouldn't leave the boat without telling me first. And why would Mr. Moran leave his shoes and jacket behind?" Clarice said in an agitated state.

"OK, folks," Captain Kerr said. "First we need to conduct a thorough search of the *Princess*. If we cannot locate them we'll have to call the police. Oh, I just thought of something. I hired a man to guard the upper deck for the evening. Part of the handrail is under repair and we didn't want to endanger any of the guests. Maybe he saw something."

"Captain, there was no one on the upper deck when we came up," Rolf said. We saw a guy leave as we were approaching the stairwell. It was probably him."

"You mean he left already? He didn't stop in for his pay. I'll have to give it to Jacobs to give to him."

"You mean the guy was a friend of Jacobs?" Rolf asked.

"Yes, Jacobs recommended him for the job."

"Do you remember his name, Captain?"

"His first name was Walter. He had a funny last name that started with a 'D,' I think."

"Would the last name be Duesterbeck?"

"Yes! That was it!"

"I think you better call the police now, Captain. I am sure we won't find the people we are looking for on the boat.

"Do you think they are in the water?" Clarice asked.

"It's the only explanation. The only reason Hank would have taken off his jacket and shoes was to jump into the river," Rolf answered.

"I'll get on the horn with the police right away," said Captain Kerr as he turned and entered the wheelhouse.

A Lansing police cruiser arrived with siren blaring and blue lights flashing ten minutes after Captain Kerr put in the call. The mere mention of a missing US senator was enough to warrant the immediate attention of the city's entire police force. The Lansing police notified the FBI field office in Detroit, but it would take them more than an hour to get to the scene.

Rolf called State Trooper Hanratty's cell number. Hanratty was just getting ready for bed when he answered.

"Trooper Hanratty, this is Rolf Kramden. I am aboard the *Lansing Princess* with Senator Westbrook's party. The senator is missing along with the Morans. I am sure Duesterbeck and his crew had something to do with their disappearance."

"Is the boat still out on the river?"

"No, we just arrived back at the dock."

"What do you think happened?"

"It looks like all three went overboard. I found Hank's jacket and shoes up on the second deck. Duesterbeck was onboard but lit out as soon as the boat docked. One of Duesterbeck's cohorts was also onboard tending bar."

"OK, Rolf, I'll be there as soon as I can!"

In the meantime a second Lansing patrol car arrived along with a dark blue Taurus carrying a pair of detectives named Ed Harrison and Jack Heath. Harrison appeared to be the lead detective as he approached the group on the gangplank.

"I'm Detective Harrison and this is Detective Heath. Would someone please tell me what in hell is going on?"

Clarice started, "I am Clarice Westbrook, wife of Senator Westbrook. My husband and two of his friends are in the river somewhere upstream!"

"How do you know this, Mrs. Westbrook?"

"They weren't on the boat when we docked," Rolf answered. "And I found this jacket and shoes up on the promenade. They belong to Mr. Hank Moran, an acquaintance of the senator's. I think there was some foul play involved."

"And who are you?" Harrison asked.

"I'm Rolf Kramden, reporter for the *Journal*."

"Oh yes, I've heard of you. In fact, I read some of your articles."

Clarice was getting highly agitated, "We don't have time to discuss newspaper articles now, Detective! You need to get some boats in the water to look for my husband!"

"Mrs. Westbrook, I alerted the river patrol right after we received Captain Kerr's emergency call. They should be deploying as we speak. Now, Mr. Kramden, tell me about this suspected foul play."

Rolf went on to explain his involvement with the Morans and the hit-and-run investigation of Jason Wengert's death. He told of the possible tie-in of the CCB and the senator's disappearance and that it was no coincidence that the group's leader and one of its members were aboard the *Princess*. He also mentioned that Jacobs was tending bar during the cruise.

Detective Harrison listened intently and then asked, "Captain Kerr, where can I find this bartender named Jacobs?"

"He should be back at the aft bar cleaning up," the captain answered.

"Jack, why don't you go round up Mr. Jacobs and escort him out here?"

"On my way, Ed."

Harrison's cell phone beeped and he paused to answer it. He appeared to be listening intently then said, "OK, glad you got in the water so fast. The area to search is from the riverboat's dock to about two miles upstream. Have one boat come downstream and the other go up. Look for three people. Two men and a woman."

Detective Heath appeared with Jacobs as Harrison was ending his call. "Ed, this is Stan Jacobs."

"Good evening, Mr. Jacobs. How is it that you happened to be tending bar tonight?"

"Captain Kerr called me and said he needed the extra help for the senator's cruise. I tend bar on the *Princess* a few times per month."

"Is that true, Captain?"

"Yes it is,Detective. Stan is a very good bartender."

"Mr. Jacobs, where is your friend Mr. Duesterbeck?"

"He left as soon as the boat docked. He told me his mother is ill and he needed to get home as soon as possible. He told me to pick up his pay that the captain promised."

"I see. Captain, how much did Mr. Duesterbeck earn this evening?"

"I told him that all I could pay was eight dollars an hour. He worked about three and a half hours, so that would be twenty eight dollars. All he had to do was stand guard and not let any of the guests up on the third deck. The handrail is under repair and I didn't want any accidents."

"He took a job that pays eight dollars an hour to guard a handrail?"

"That is correct, Detective. Stan here recommended him."

"Mr. Jacobs, Why would a man like Duesterbeck take a job that paid eight dollars an hour? Surely he doesn't need the money."

"When I told him about it he said he would do it just for something to do. He needed a break from tending to his sick mother."

"It's too bad Mr. Duesterbeck had to run off. He might have seen something from his station on the upper deck. Jack, get with the station and have Mr. Duesterbeck picked up for questioning."

"I can take care of that," came a voice from behind Harrison.

Harrison turned around and saw Trooper Hanratty standing behind him. "Hanratty," Harrison said, "What are you doing out on this fine evening?

"Mr. Kramden called earlier and told me what was happening so I thought I'd stop by."

"Did I hear you say you can pick up Duesterbeck?

"That's right. He owns a farm over in Barry County and is most likely headed there now."

"Well, in that case, I'm glad you showed up. Barry County is well out of our jurisdiction."

"We need to pick him up for questioning in another matter, so I am glad to be of service. I'll get right on it."

"Shouldn't we call the Barry County sheriff and have him pick up Mr. Duesterbeck?" Harrison said.

"I think it is a wise move to leave the sheriff out of this for the moment," Hanratty said.

"Uh huh, well then I'll leave the roundup of Mr. Duesterbeck in your hands, Trooper."

Hanratty said he'd get on it right away and left.

Harrison's cell phone beeped.

Harrison here . . . I see. Only one?. . . Uh huh . . . OK, keep me posted."

After ending his call he turned to the group, "The river patrol found an empty boat grounded on a sandbar about two miles upstream. The outboard engine was still running. The other patrol boat reported that they found a man's body floating a mile upstream."

After hearing the report, Clarice swooned but steadied herself against the captain.

Harrison added, "They will call as soon as they retrieve the body and get a better look at it."

Thirty minutes earlier

Hank and the senator had drifted with the current about a quarter mile since they had entered the water. They approached a section of the river where a residential area lined one side. The ambient light from the nearby houses was enough for Hank to make out the north bank, which seemed to be only thirty yards away.

Hank saw a sweeping light, which appeared to be in a search mode. His first thought was that Helen had alerted the captain and that their rescue was forthcoming. "Hang on a little longer, Senator. It looks like help is on the way," Hank said

As the light bearer approached Hank could see there was one man in a small outboard. He waived and shouted toward the boat and then the strong light shone directly on them. Hank had to shield his eyes to prevent being blinded by the beam's intensity. He heard the outboard motor accelerate and saw the boat pick up speed and head directly toward them.

When the boat was ten feet away it veered slightly to Hank's right to prevent running directly over them. As the boat sped past the driver stood up and with one hand swung a wooden oar with the malevolent intent of hitting them. Luckily his aim was off and the oar hit the water inches from Hank's head. The man lost his grip on the oar due to the impact with the water and he lost it overboard.

"Dammit, Hank," the senator said. "I do believe that gentleman has hostile intentions."

"Not only that, Senator, I think he's trying to kill us."

Hank saw the oar floating five feet away and managed to paddle to it as he heard the boat turn and head back in their direction. "Senator, my feet just hit bottom! See if you can stand!"

"Yes, I feel the bottom!"

"OK, now stay behind me on the bank side. The boat is coming back fast. We won't have time to make it to the bank before he makes another pass at us."

Hank managed to get a firm foothold with water up to his chest just as the boat was twenty feet away. He saw the man stand up with another oar in his hand. Hank was ready as he anticipated the boatman would veer to his right once again. Like a knight in a jousting contest, Hank quickly raised and extended his oar and thrust with perfect timing, catching the boatman square in the chest.

Hank heard a sickening crunch as the oar made contact. There was a simultaneous grunt and "oomph," and the sound of a rapid expulsion of air as the boatman reeled backwards off the far side of the boat, followed by a large splash as the body hit the water. The now empty boat sped past. Fortunately, Hank's arm absorbed most of the force and he was only sent underwater a brief second.

The boat continued on its own to parts unknown. Apparently the motor's deadman line was not hooked to the boat's lone occupant. Hank could hear no other splashing or struggling in the water and figured the boatman was unconscious and drifting down river. "Sorry, fella. I'm in no mood for another swim tonight," Hank said as he followed the senator ashore.

Luck was with them as the encounter with the boatman took place on an inside bend of the river where the water was normally shallower and the current not as strong. With the help of some tree roots and low hanging branches, Hank managed to help the senator to the top of the eight foot river bank.

Hank and Senator Westbrook decided to sit for a while until the senator regained his senses. "Maybe we should have headed for the bank over there," Hank said. Looks like a lot of houses. We sure could use a phone. Nothing on this side of the river but woods."

"We can't be more than a mile or two upstream from the boat dock," Westbrook said. "As soon as my head clears we'll just have to start walking."

"Senator, you can talk all you want about walking. You still have your shoes."

"Maybe I can loan you one of mine and we could kinda hop along."

"No thanks, Senator, I don't think I could fill even one of your shoes. And while we're sitting here, tell me what in hell happened to you."

"Well, I was standing near the bar talking to some friends when the bartender asked to have a word with me. I walked over to him and he said the captain wanted to see me up in the wheelhouse. When I got up to the top deck I met a guy who I quickly found out was Duesterbeck. He gave me all this stuff about the evil of gun control and wanted me to kill the legislation I authored on tightening registration for automatic weapons. When I told him I would do no such thing, I was hit on the head and dumped overboard. I must have been out cause I don't remember the fall, but I came to as soon as I hit the river. I was swallowing a lot of water and could barely manage to keep my head above water when you rescued me."

"Hmm. We figured Duesterbeck had something big planned, and it looks like you were it," Hank said. "He planned to dump you overboard and have one of his cronies in a boat make sure you drowned. If they played it right it would have looked like you were drunk and accidentally fell overboard. If Helen and I hadn't been up on the promenade and have seen you fall right in front of our noses their plan might have worked."

"Somehow they knew I was a serious scotch drinker. That damned bartender kept giving me double shots of some good twelve year old."

"Well, Senator, let's get up and start walking. Our wives must be worried sick about us by now."

"Hank, you saved my life tonight. How can I ever repay you?"

"Senator, if you remember correctly, I owe you one. Let's just call it even."

Chapter 10

Helen was in complete darkness as the tarp-covered boat and trailer bounced along the country roads. Carter had apparently decided to stick to the secondary roads for the fifty mile trip back to Duesterbeck's farm.

Lying on her side, Helen was free to explore the area of the boat behind her. Her fingers found what she believed to be the bottom edge of the formed and riveted sheet aluminum boat seat. The edge felt sharp enough for her intended purpose.

After sliding her back closer to the seat, she had to get into an awkward position in order to place the portion of the tape that was between her wrists onto the sharp edge of the seat bottom. The bouncing of the boat trailer made her lose the position numerous times, but finally she could feel the fabric embedded in the tape start to give way.

One hard bounce of the trailer aided in the final tearing of the tape. Helen peeled the tape from her wrists and started working on the tape that was wrapped around her mouth and head. The only trouble was the tape over Helen's mouth was in numerous layers. She felt around to the back and sides of her head and found some of the wraps were spread out in a single ply.

Helen made short work of the tape and gingerly pulled it away from her face and hair. "I hope there's more hair left on my head than on the tape," she said to herself as the last piece of tape came free. The tape binding her ankles was an easier task, and she was quickly able to tear and unwrap it.

Free from the duct tape Helen was able to move into a position to lift the edge of the tarp and peer over the gunwale.

She didn't want to lift it too high, as she didn't know how clearly Carter could see the boat in his rearview mirrors. The half moon was just coming up bright and cast its light on the passing corn fields. Helen thought about jumping out of the moving trailer, but she figured she would only get injured and that Carter would find her, knock her out with the chloroform, and put her back in the boat. She decided she would have to take her chances when the rig stopped.

Detective Harrison continued his questioning of Stan Jacobs. "Mr. Jacobs, did you notice how much Senator Westbrook had to drink tonight?"

"He drank quite a lot. I had a bottle of single malt scotch and he kept coming back for double shots over ice."

"Then, would you say that by the time he went among the missing he was feeling quite high?"

"Yes, I would say that. He was quite unsteady as he walked toward the stairwell."

"Jacobs, where did you get a bottle of single malt scotch?" Captain Kerr asked. "I don't recall having a high priced liquor like that on board."

"Some guy handed it to me and said it was strictly for the senator's consumption, that it was his favorite drink. I assumed it was from one of his political donors."

"Where is the bottle of scotch now?" Harrison asked.

"The senator asked for the bottle and then headed for the stairwell. I assumed he was headed up to see the captain."

Harrison's cell phone beeped once again. He said, "Excuse me. I have to take this call. Harrison! Uh huh . . . handlebar mustache? What was the name again? Gotcha. Keep looking. There's still three unaccounted for."

Harrison disconnected from the call and faced Mrs. Westbrook. "The body they found in the river was not your husband's, Mrs. Westbrook."

"Please tell me it wasn't Hank Moran," Rolf said.

"It wasn't Mr. Moran either. The driver's license found in the wallet in the back pocket belonged to a Mr. Harry Griggs. Body had the same handlebar mustache as on his license photo.

"That's the third member of the CCB in the area tonight," Rolf said. "Two on the *Princess* and one on the river. I think Mr. Jacobs here knows a little more about what happened to the senator than he is letting on."

"I've told you all I know," Jacobs said. "Am I free to go now?"

"Mr. Jacobs, what was the brand name of that twelve year old scotch the senator was drinking?"

"It was Macallan. Why do you ask?"

"The river patrol found it floating in the river. You may go back to your cleanup duties, Mr. Jacobs, but don't leave this boat until I say you can."

On his way back to the bar Jacobs pulled out his cell phone and tapped Duesterbeck's speed dial number.

Duesterbeck answered on the third ring. "Duesterbeck."

"Major, this is Jacobs."

"Jacobs, I know it's you. How many times do I have to tell you I have caller ID?

"Major, they found Griggs's body in the river. Dead."

"They only found his?"

"So far that's all they found. Him and the scotch bottle. Nothing on the senator or Moran as of yet."

"Well shit, shit, SHIT! If Griggs is dead, chances are either the senator or Moran or both of them are still alive. If Moran and the senator are dead, it can still look like the drunken fool fell overboard and the Morans drowned trying to save him. If one of them is still alive, we're screwed. Jacobs, stick around there and let me know as soon as anything else becomes known."

"I have to stay here. The detectives won't let me leave."

"OK, I'm on my way to the farm to see what to do about the Moran woman."

"What are you going to do with her?"

"I don't know yet. Depends on what happens back there. If we get lucky and they find two more bodies, we might have to take her back to the river and dispose of her."

Hank and Senator Westbrook started their trek back to the *Princess*'s dock. "Hank, if we head straight out from the river we should come to the Old Lansing Road. It follows pretty close to the river."

"Sounds like a plan, Senator. My feet will last a lot longer on a paved road. Good thing there are lots of leaves here to step on."

"My heart bleeds for you and your feet, Hank."

"No more talk about bleeding, Senator.Let's go, but take it easy."

Ten minutes later they could see a street light through the trees. "That must be the road straight ahead, Hank."

"Let's keep moving, Senator. So far I'm doing OK. Us southern boys spend a lot of time barefoot and develop a tough hide."

"Hell, Hank, I get a little pebble in my shoe and I'm yelping."

"Yeah, I always figured you Yankees were a bunch of softies."

"Ouch, now that remark hurt, Hank."

"It probably didn't hurt as much as my feet will if I don't get some shoes on soon," Hank said with a chuckle.

When they reached the Old Lansing Road they found themselves facing a residential area across the road. "Civilization at last!" Hank said as they scanned the houses.

"That house over there still has lights on," Westbrook said. "Let's go over and knock."

The bedraggled pair made it across the road with Hank trying to light step it across the graveled berm. "Damn that hurts," he expounded in agony. The house's lush front lawn was a welcome relief.

Upon approaching the front door Hank waved his hand in a "be my guest" gesture for the senator to proceed and knock on the door. "You go ahead, Senator. A bullet came through the last door I knocked on when I was in your company."

"Thanks, Hank, you're all heart," Westbrook said as he grinned and knocked.

They heard footsteps and the porch light came on. The white lace curtain parted on the front door and a young girl's face appeared. "Dad, there's two men at the door."

"Don't open it! I'll get my gun," a man's voice said.

Out of force of habit, Hank nudged the Senator to the left side of the door and he took up position on the right side.

One minute later the curtain parted again and a man's face appeared. "What do you fellas want? I'm armed!" said the man.

"Mister, we don't mean any harm to you or your family. I am Senator Kenton Westbrook and I need to use your phone."

"Riiight. And I'm President George H.W. Bush. You don't look like no senator to me. You look like a pair of bums. Now get movin on."

"Sir, please. Just call 911 and tell the dispatcher that Senator Westbrook is at your front door. We'll wait out front on the lawn."

"Dad! I just saw the news on TV. They said Senator Westbrook is missing and they showed his picture. He sure looks like the guy out front."

"OK, my daughter said she just saw you on the news. I'll call 911 like you said, but I ain't invitin you in. I voted against you the last time. Just so you know."

"That's perfectly OK, sir. Please make that call. We'll be more than happy to wait out here."

Additional police officers had arrived on the scene and Harrison put them to work searching the *Princess* for the three missing persons. Detective Heath proceeded to question the remaining guests that had not made it off the boat before the police arrived.

The searchers on the *Princess* found a purse in a dark corner of the third deck at the top of the stairwell, but there was no sign of the missing trio. The questioning of the remaining passengers proved fruitless. No one had noticed what had happened to the senator.

Detective Heath checked the contents of the purse and found that it belonged to Helen Moran. The purse contained a small wallet with her driver's license, makeup, and a cell phone. He had just reported the find back to Harrison when Harrison's cell phone beeped again.

Harrison glanced at the incoming number and saw it was from the 911 dispatcher and answered it. "Harrison. Are you sure? No, don't do that, I'll head up there myself."

"Mrs. Westbrook, that was the 911 dispatcher. A caller who lives a mile and a half upriver on Old Lansing Road claims your husband and another man are waiting out front on his lawn. He seemed sure that one of them was your husband. Detective Heath and I are heading up there now."

"I'm coming with you!" Clarice said.

"I am sorry, but there won't be room for all of us in the car for the ride back. I'll tell you what. I'll have one of the patrol cars follow us. You can ride with him."

"Did they say if Mrs. Moran was with them?" Rolf asked.

"No, they just said it was two men."

Helen felt the trailer slow and make a turn. She recognized the brick entrance facade and iron gate of Duesterbeck's farm when she lifted the tarp slightly to peek over the gunwale. *Looks like it's showtime,* she thought.

Carter made the turn into Duesterbeck's driveway, bypassed the house, and stopped in front of the barn. *Don't want to wake his old lady,* he thought. *The major would be pissed.* He exited his truck and then reached back in for the bottle of chloroform on the front seat. He had laid the old towel that Duesterbeck used with the chloroform on the floor behind the passenger seat. He didn't want any of the fumes from the rag to knock him out while he was driving, and just to play safe, he made the trip with the windows open. He walked around the truck to the passenger side to retrieve the old towel.

Helen heard the doors open and close on the truck and was sure she heard the passenger side door shut last. She anticipated that Carter would lift the tarp from the same side of the boat. She positioned herself on her back as quietly as she could with her feet facing the starboard side. She drew her right knee up tight against her chest, braced herself with her hands and left foot, and waited.

As Carter walked back to the boat he sensed the quiet. "The lady must still be out,"he mumbled to himself. "Better give her another shot of this stuff just to play safe."

The moon was rising behind the barn casting the barn's shadow upon the truck and boat trailer. The contrast made it difficult for him to find the tarp tie-downs. He fumbled with the tie-downs and managed to unfasten them starting on the bow and working his way back to the transom.

He picked up the bottle of chloroform he had placed on the trailer frame near the hitch and poured some onto the rag being careful not to breathe in any stray fumes.

He walked back to the middle of the trailer and, holding the rag in one hand, he flipped the tarp back with the other. All he could make out was the lady's form in the dark bottom of the boat so he leaned in a bit closer for a better look.

Hank and Senator Westbrook were sitting on the front lawn patiently waiting. The senator was about to get up and go knock on the door again when they saw the blue lights coming up the road. They both stood up and waved their arms above their heads to flag down the approaching vehicles.

The blue Taurus was in the lead followed by a police cruiser. When the vehicles stopped in front of them Clarice bounded out of the cruiser and ran to her husband. She flew into his arms and nearly knocked him over.

Hank looked towards the police cruiser and stood in anticipation of Helen doing likewise, but then realized there were no other passengers. A feeling of dread overtook him. He knew there was no way Helen would have stayed behind on the *Princess* unless she had been harmed in some way.

Harrison recognized the senator and then turned towards Hank. "I'm Detective Harrison, and you must be Mr. Moran."

"Yes, I am," Hank answered.

"Looks like you two had some ordeal this evening. Are you both OK? Do we need to call an ambulance?" Harrison asked.

"We're both fine," Hank answered. "We're a little waterlogged, but we're OK. The senator received a blow on the head but he seems to have fully recovered."

"We'll have the EMTs check him out when we get back to the boat."

"Sounds good, Detective. I want to get back to my wife, Helen. She must be worried sick about me."

"Mr. Moran, I'm sorry to have to tell you this, but your wife is not back at the boat. We thought she was with you."

"No, she was not with us!" Hank said, starting to show signs of panic. "When I jumped into the river after the senator she was headed up to the wheelhouse to alert the captain!"

"I am afraid she never made it to the wheelhouse, Mr. Moran. We made a thorough search of the boat and only found her purse. The marine patrol still has two boats out searching the river. So far they only found one body and that belonged to a Harry Griggs."

"Let's get back to the boat! I need to look for Helen!" Hank shouted in panic and despair.

On the short ride back to the boat, Hank tried to put the thoughts of Duesterbeck harming Helen and dumping her in the river out of his mind. Somehow he knew she was going to be OK.

Word spread rapidly around the boat that the senator and Hank Moran had been found alive. On hearing the news Jacobs immediately called Duesterbeck. Duesterbeck answered the call and listened, "Major, it's Jacobs."

"Dammit, Jacobs, how many times must I tell you I have caller . . . forget it. What happened?"

"They found both Westbrook and Moran alive."

There was a pregnant pause and then Duesterbeck ended the call on his smartphone with a tap of his finger.

Harrison quickly found out from the senator that Duesterbeck and the bartender had knocked him out and dumped him in the river. He radioed the officers at the boat and told them to place Jacobs under immediate arrest.

By the time the two vehicles made it back to the boat, Jacobs was in cuffs in the backseat of a patrol car. He had tried to take advantage of the absence of Harrison and Heath by trying to slip past the group at the entrance to the gangplank. Jacobs tried to casually walk down the gangplank, hoping he would be inconspicuous. Harrison's call was timely and an officer spotted Jacobs, shouted his name, and ran towards him. Jacobs tried to take off and run but tripped on the end of the gangplank and fell into the officer's grip. He was then pinned down and cuffed.

Hank rode in the patrol car while the Westbrooks rode the short distance back to the *Princess* in Harrison's Taurus. Upon reaching the boat Harrison immediately asked, "Where's Jacobs?"

An officer named Carlson responded, "He's cuffed in the back of my patrol car. Do you want me to take him downtown?"

"Not yet. We'll question him here. Did you read him his rights?"

"Yes, sir. Said he didn't want a lawyer. Claims he didn't do anything wrong."

"I have a feeling he'll soon change his mind. Take him into the boat and sit him at one of the tables. I'll be there in a minute."

Harrison remembered that Trooper Hanratty was on his way to Duesterbeck's farm to bring him in for questioning. He located Rolf and got Hanratty's cell phone number.

Hanratty had his phone synced to his cruiser and answered Harrison's call with the button on his steering wheel. "Bill Hanratty."

"Bill, this is Detective Harrison. The situation has changed. Duesterbeck needs to be arrested and brought in on the charge of attempted murder of Senator Westbrook. Don't try to do it alone. You are going to need backup."

"Thanks for the heads up, Ed. I'll radio for the posse."

"Be careful, Bill. He'll most likely be A and D."

"Yeah, most likely. We'll try to avoid another Waco, Ed."

Harrison finished his call to Hanratty and headed towards the gangplank. As he approached the group at the dock he said, "Senator, I need you and Mr. Moran to follow me." He nodded for Detective Heath to join them.

Rolf tapped Hank on his shoulder and said, "Hank, you might want these," as he held out Hank's shoes, jacket, and wallet.

"Thanks, Rolf. And my feet thank you. I'll be right in as soon as I dress, Detective."

Jacobs was seated at a large round table with a uniformed officer posted on each side of him. Harrison dismissed the two officers as the group approached the table.

"You guys can take a break now, but stick around. You'll need to escort Mr. Jacobs here to the downtown lockup a bit later."

Harrison sat two seats to the right of Jacobs, and Heath two seats to the left. Westbrook and Hank took chairs directly across from Jacobs.

"All right, Mr. Jacobs," Harrison started. "It's time to talk. I understand you have been read your rights and refused counsel at this time. Is that correct?"

"That's right. I didn't do anything to need a lawyer for."

"We beg to differ with you, Mr. Jacobs. The senator here said you knocked him over the head and you and Walter Duesterbeck dumped him overboard into the river."

"That's bullshit. How would he know it was me? His back was tur—"

"Were you going to say his back was turned to you, Mr. Jacobs?"

The exchange produced grins from everyone at the table except Jacobs.

"If you knew the senator's back was turned to you that means you were involved in the attempted murder. Weren't you, Mr. Jacobs?"

"I ain't sayin anything else. I want a lawyer."

"Detective Harrison, can I say something?" Westbrook asked.

"Go ahead, Senator."

"Jacobs had called me aside at the bar and told me that the captain wanted to speak with me up in the wheelhouse. I proceeded up the stairwell and heard someone behind me. I turned and saw Jacobs. There was no one else with him. He also took part in the conversation I had with Duesterbeck. It was only the three of us up on the top deck."

"It seems we have you dead to right, Mr. Jacobs," Harrison said. "The attempted murder of a US senator is good for at least thirty years in the federal pen. It might go a little easier on you if you open up and tell us exactly what took place."

"What does that mean? What do you mean by a little easier?" Jacobs asked.

"I am sure we can convince the prosecutor to push for a lighter sentence if you are totally cooperative. There is also the matter of the disappearance of Mrs. Helen Moran. Conspiracy to kidnap is also a serious crime. If you don't cooperate you will most likely spend the rest of your life in prison as Big Bubba's plaything."

Jacobs was silent, apparently pondering his options. Harrison saw Hank glaring at Jacobs with malice in his eyes and had an idea.

"Perhaps we should let you alone with Mr. Moran here for a while," Harrison said. "He is extremely anxious to learn what happened to his wife. Mr. Moran is a homicide detective from down in Louisiana. I understand that down in Louisiana they have special ways of making people talk. Isn't that right, Mr. Moran?"

"All I would need is five minutes and a pair of pliers from the boat's toolbox," Hank said.

Jacobs quickly looked up to see Hank glaring at him. A moment later he said, "All right, the woman should be OK. The major just knocked her out with a rag full of some stuff he had poured from a bottle."

"Where is she now?" Hank asked gritting his teeth.

"We loaded her in Carter's boat. He was supposed to take her out to the farm. I don't know what the major plans to do with her."

Hank immediately bolted from the table and headed towards the exit. Harrison shouted, "Moran! Where are you going?"

Hank didn't answer and ran down the gangplank. In passing he shouted to Rolf, "Duesterbeck's farm!"

"Hold it, Hank. I'm going with you," Rolf shouted.

Rolf turned to his fiancée, reached into his pocket, and tossed her his car keys. "Take my car to get home. I have to go with Hank."

Rolf turned and ran after Hank. He caught up to him just as the Honda's engine came to life and he managed to jump into the passenger seat as Hank hit reverse.

"Just get us there alive, Hank. I'll give you directions for the quickest way. And keep an eye out for deer. They'll be out foraging this time of night."

Harrison immediately called Trooper Hanratty. "Bill, this is Harrison. How close are you to the farm?"

"I'm about ten miles out with the posse about two minutes behind."

"We just learned that Mrs. Moran could be being held there in a hostage situation. Things are getting touchy."

"Oh man, you said it. We'll proceed with all the necessary caution."

"Another thing, her husband is on the way out there with blood in his eyes."

"Damn. That's all we need."

As Harrison was ending the call to Hanratty he noticed a large sedan pull up and two men get out sporting FBI jackets.

"We're looking for Detective Harrison," the shorter stocky one said.

"I'm Harrison. What took you guys so long?"

Harrison knew that with the attempted murder of a US senator and subsequent kidnapping the FBI would be running the show from now on. He dreaded the idea of having to take the time to bring them up to speed.

Chapter 11

Helen tensed as the tarp was flipped back off the boat. She could see Carter's upper half silhouetted against the brightening moonlit sky. When he seemed to lean forward in her direction she thought, *Now or never,* and thrust her right leg up and caught him square on the nose with the heel of her shoe. Helen heard the splat of crushed nose cartilage.

Carter yelped like a hound dog, dropped the chloroform laced towel into the boat, grabbed for his nose, and tried to straighten up. He didn't quite make it as Helen reached up with two hands, grabbed the hair on the back of his head, and pulled down with all her might. Carter's mouth was forced down onto the boats gunwale with the sickening sound of teeth hitting metal. She remembered her self-defense instructor saying "Once you have him down, make sure he doesn't get back up." Helen pulled forward so that Carter's neck was over the gunwale and put her upper body weight on the back of his head. She reached down for the chloroformed towel and with one hand held it beneath her and against Carter's mouth and nose. "Here fella, this may stop the bleeding," she said as she waited for either chloroform or lack of air to overcome the man.

Helen felt Carter go limp but held on for another ten to fifteen seconds to make sure he was out; it was only an hour or two ago that she had played possum herself.

Being satisfied that he was unconscious she pushed him off the side of the boat and eased herself over the gunwale on the opposite side. It felt good to get her feet on solid ground once again.

Helen paused to look around and get her bearings. She could see the farmhouse but no lights were on inside. Apparently Duesterbeck's mother was in bed. She didn't want to approach the old lady, not knowing if she was involved with the CCB or not. Surely she would be defensive when it came to her son. She needed to call Hank to find out if he was all right and to let him know where she was. She decided to check Carter and his truck to see if he had a cell phone.

As she was walking around to the other side of the boat where Carter laid, she saw car lights slow out on the road and turn into the driveway.

She figured the best thing to do was to get out of sight on the back side of the barn and then keep going. When she got far enough away she could circle around to the road and maybe flag someone down. Although anyone driving around at this time of night, she realized, might be a CCB member helping in the search for her.

Helen quickly circled around the barn and found a hard packed tractor lane leading straight out away from the barn. *I don't know where it leads,* she thought, *but anywhere away from here is good. It's hard packed, too. I won't leave many tracks.*

Duesterbeck turned into his drive and sped down the quarter mile long driveway. He bypassed the house and came to a halt behind Carter's truck and boat trailer. He left his Escalade running with the lights on and exited the vehicle.

Carter was nowhere in sight. He peered into the boat and saw it was empty. *He must have taken her into the barn,* he thought. Then he heard a moan from the other side of the boat. "Carter! Is that you?" Another moan was the response.

Duesterbeck walked around to the other side of the boat just as Carter was struggling to sit up. "What in the hell happened to you? You look like you were in a brawl," Duesterbeck said.

"I was attacked by a damned wild woman. I think she broke my nose and knocked some of my teeth loose."

"How the fuck could a woman her size do something like that to you?"

"I don't know, Major. It all happened so fast. I took the tarp off the boat to give her another shot of chloroform and all hell broke loose. Next thing I remember I was coming to and you were standing there. Damn, my throat hurts, too. Feels like she crushed my Adam's apple."

"She must have taken off. It doesn't make any difference now anyways. I guess you haven't heard. Griggs is dead and Westbrook and Moran are alive. By now they have Jacobs in custody and he's probably singing like a canary on poppy seeds trying to save himself."

"What are we going to do, Major?"

"You're on your own, Carter. I suggest that you get out of here as quick as you can. The police can't be far behind."

Carter struggled to his feet then unhitched the boat trailer from his truck. "I'm gonna head out the back way, Major. Cops will probably come in from the front."

"Good idea! I have to take care of something in the house then I'll be right behind you," Duesterbeck said.

He jumped back into the Escalade, shifted into reverse and hit the gas. Stopping in front of his house, he ran inside leaving the big SUV running with its door open.

"Walter, is that you?" his mother called in a weak voice.

"Yes it is, Mother. Go back to sleep. I don't have time to talk now."

Duesterbeck, in his haste, fumbled with the combination to his wall safe. After three frustrating tries and a tirade of cussing he managed to open it and stick wads of cash into a bank moneybag, then head back outside. He tossed the moneybag onto the passenger seat, jumped into the Escalade, shifted into all-wheel drive and headed back towards the barn.

Inside the barn he removed a padlock and entered a storeroom, which had been refurbished into a small but well-stocked armory. The weapons, having been accumulated over the past ten years, ranged from a pair of small .22 caliber revolvers to three light anti-tank AT4's.

He pulled a Colt M1911 semi-auto .45 caliber handgun and an AR-15 automatic rifle off the display wall, grabbed a box of ammo for each weapon off the storage shelf, and headed back outside. Not even stopping to padlock the armory door, he was back in the Escalade and speeding down the dirt track away from the back of the barn, hoping to run into his escaped hostage for future leverage.

Helen walked rapidly down the dirt tractor path and came to an area that looked like an old movie set. It was easy to make out the facades of four structures in the brightening moonlight. She remembered Rolf speaking of these buildings that the Battalion used to practice urban warfare.

She heard a rumble and turned to see the lights of a vehicle coming towards her. She was sure the driver had not yet seen her in his headlights so she ran the thirty yards to the first building front and managed to duck behind the open doorway just as the truck's lights illuminated the area.

She recognized Carter's red truck and thought sure he had revived and had come looking for her. She was about to take off running out the back of the small complex when she realized the truck was not stopping and blew on by in a cloud of dust.

Not wanting to risk being seen on the tractor path, Helen began walking away from the complex along the grassy edge of a cornfield. The corn was lush with the stalks towering over her head. The cornstalks were just starting to show signs of turning brown, readying themselves for the October harvest. Walking along the cornfield brought back memories of her childhood playing hide and seek on her grandfather's farm in northern Louisiana. She knew that if she had to she could duck into the cornfield and her pursuers would have an extremely difficult time of finding her, especially at night.

She anticipated that once she got to the edge of the cornfield she could turn the corner and follow the other edge of the corn out to the road. She remembered seeing the cornfield when, only yesterday, Rolf had taken the route past Duesterbeck's farm on the way to the hit-and-run scene.

She was well out of sight of the farmhouse and barn, but thought she heard another vehicle come down the tractor lane, which was now about a hundred yards away.

Duesterbeck slowed as he approached the urban warfare practice area. He had seen that a few of her tracks led down the tractor lane and thought the buildings ahead would make good hiding places for her. He stopped in front of the practice area and exited the Escalade to examine the grounds with a flashlight. He found some faint tracks that looked like the woman's entering the area, but the woman was nowhere to be found. The dirt in the practice area was packed hard and no exit tracks could be found.

As Helen neared the end of the cornfield she could hear a police siren out on the road that seemed to stop, she guessed, near the entrance to the farm. She entertained the thought of heading back to the farmhouse, but gave it up when she realized that it could be a sheriff's deputy or Sheriff Engle himself, arriving to help Duesterbeck. *I better keep on heading straight and parallel to the road to get farther away,* she thought. She looked around and spotted a bouncing light approaching from the direction of the practice facades.

A mile away from the farm Trooper Hanratty cut his siren and proceeded in silence the rest of the way. He was the first officer to arrive at the entrance to Duesterbeck's farm and found the gate open. He drove slowly down the tree lined drive with his lights out. As he neared the farmhouse he could see no other vehicles. He saw what appeared to be an aluminum boat and trailer down in front of the barn.

Hanratty heard his backup state police car coming down the road with its siren at full blast. In less than a minute the patrol car came barreling down the lane and stopped behind him. "I heard you coming two miles out," an obviously irritated Hanratty told Trooper Haddix.

"Sorry, Bill," he answered, "but I wanted to make sure the deer were scared out of my path. Hitting one doing eighty would make an awful mess of my car and me."

"Well, no harm done, Jim. It appears they already cleared out."

Just then the front porch light came on and an elderly lady in a nightgown appeared pointing a shotgun in their direction. "What's all this racket out here? What do you fellas want? Don't you know it's the middle of the night? If you weren't the police, I'd put a load of birdshot up your backsides. Disturbing an old woman's sleep."

"Sorry for the disturbance, ma'am, but we are looking for Walter Duesterbeck," Hanratty said.

"Well you can look all you want but my son ain't here."

"Have you seen him this evening, Mrs. Duesterbeck?

"I didn't see him, but I heard him come in. He was only here a few minutes and left. Told me he didn't have time to talk. Looks like he took money out of the safe and left it standing wide open. Anyone could have come in and cleaned us out. Why are you looking for Walter?"

"The Lansing police are looking for him. We believe he was involved in the attempted murder of Senator Westbrook earlier this evening."

"You said attempted murder? Too bad. That means that S.O.B. is still alive."

"Yes, I am glad to report the senator is fine, ma'am. Would you please step aside? We need to search the house."

"I told you he ain't here."

"Ma'am, we need to check just to be sure. He may be in there without your knowledge."

"Well then, make it quick and don't wreck the joint or I'll sue the britches off ya."

The two troopers had completed a search of the house and grounds and were walking toward the barn when they heard a car speeding down the drive. The gray Honda came to a stop beside Haddix's patrol car and Hank and Rolf got out and strode toward them. Haddix shouted, "Stop right there," while drawing his service revolver.

"It's all right, Jim. They're friendlies," Hanratty shouted. "That's Hank Moran, the guy who saved the senator from drowning in the river. And the other guy is Rolf Kramden from the *Journal*. How in the hell did they get here so fast?"

"Any sign of Duesterbeck?" Hank asked as he approached the two troopers.

"His mother claimed he was here earlier and then left. We searched the house and the grounds and were just heading to the barn when you arrived. I think she is telling the truth as there are no other vehicles around. There is a boat on a trailer down in front of the barn that we need to take a look at."

Hank trotted back to the Honda, retrieved a flashlight, and said, "Let's go check that boat."

Hank jogged down to the boat well in front of the small group. He shined his light into the boat hoping to see Helen, but the first thing that caught his eye was a small bloody towel. Hank picked up the towel and could detect the sweet acetone-like odor of chloroform. Aiming his light once again into the boat he saw the torn pieces of gray duct tape scattered across the bottom.

A glint of shiny metal caught his eye. He turned over a piece of the duct tape and saw Helen's T.C.B. bracelet stuck to it. "Trooper Hanratty! You better take a picture of this before I remove it!"

Hanratty strode up to beside Hank and said, "What did you find?"

"That's Helen's bracelet stuck to that piece of tape. I'm taking it with me after you get a picture of it. I'm going into the barn to look for her."

"Hank, slow down. Jim and I are going in first. You and Rolf wait here till we give you the all clear."

"Sorry, Trooper, but I'm going in right behind you," Hank replied. "Helen could be in there. We're wasting time."

The two troopers, not wanting to take time to argue, drew their revolvers and headed through the small barn door that was mounted within one of the large double doors. Once inside, Hanratty stepped to the left and Haddix to the right. With their weapons at the ready they shined their lights around the barn.

Hank waited briefly outside, and after hearing no gunfire or shouts, went through the door.

"Not much in here, only one small tractor," Hanratty said.

Hank shined his light around and noticed what appeared to be a walled off room. "Let's go check that out," he said.

As Hank approached the door to the room he noticed the padlock just hanging in the clasp. Lifting the lock free he opened the door and called, "Helen, are you in here?" He received no response as he shined his light around. He found a light switch next to the door and flipped it on.

The two troopers and Rolf stepped into the room behind Hank, and they all stood in amazement at the copious display of weaponry lining the walls. A homemade but well crafted poster was pinned to the only weapon free spot on the wall.

It read:

Thank God for:

Fox News,
Rush Limbaugh,
and the US Military

"So, Fox News and Rush Limbaugh take the top two spots in these guys' prayers? Hmpf." Rolf said.

"Luckily this is only the mantra of a small few who can't think for themselves, and not the national sentiment." Hanratty replied.

"You may think it's only a small few. Both have large followings," Hank added

"I am sure our friends from the ATF will find this room very interesting," Hanratty said.

"We could stand and look at this all night, but this isn't finding Helen," Hank replied

"They must have taken her with them," Haddix said.

"What I can't understand is all the duct tape in the boat. Surely they would have kept her bound up," Rolf said.

"The boat was covered by a tarp," Hank replied. "If she was bound up with the tape they probably kept her in the boat while it was being trailered out here. My guess is she came to and freed herself of the tape on the way. What happened when they arrived here is anybody's guess. I don't want to think about whose blood is on the chloroformed rag and on the top edge of the boat."

"Does anybody know what vehicles they drive?" Hanratty asked.

"Duesterbeck has a black Escalade and Carter drives a red Dodge Ram 4WD," Rolf answered.

"I'll get back to my car and put out a statewide APB," Hanratty said. "In the meantime, you three search the grounds around the barn."

"Trooper Hanratty, I'll follow you back to the boat," Hank said. "I need you to take those pictures."

After posting the alerts from his patrol car, Hanratty arrived back at the boat with a camera in hand. He took three snapshots of the tape in the bottom of the boat, then gave Hank permission to retrieve Helen's bracelet. Hank carefully removed the bracelet from the tacky tape and placed it in his pocket.

"I'm going to check around the grounds for footprints," Hank said. "If Helen had revived it means she would have been on foot and could have left some prints. She was wearing a pair of wedges and her prints should be easy to distinguish from a man's shoe."

"You go ahead," Hanratty said, "I'm going back to the house to further question Mrs. Duesterbeck."

Hank slowly circled the boat with his light finding a few bare patches of ground in the six inch high grass. He was able to distinguish two smaller footprints that held promise. Upon examining a larger bare patch on the left side of the barn he found a set of footprints he was sure were Helen's. The footprints led towards the back of the barn. There were no larger footprints, only two sets of tire tracks.

Hank tried to make sense of what he was seeing.

A portion of Helen's prints appeared to be overrun by the tire tracks. A footprint here and there led to the rear of the barn and onto a dirt tractor lane. Once again some of what he was sure were Helen's footprints were overrun with tire tracks. Hank ran back to the barn to alert Rolf as to what he found. The two then followed the tractor lane and the combination of tracks to the urban warfare facades where Helen's footprints seemingly ended. There were some larger men's footprints that appeared to overlap some of Helen's.

Hank's heart sank as it appeared that Helen was on foot, then chased down by the vehicles and recaptured.

They searched around the false front buildings calling her name but to no avail.

"We have to get back to the house and find out where this path leads from here," Hank said. "It looks like the vehicles kept going. The tread marks indicate the vehicles only moved in one direction, straight ahead."

Hanratty was exiting the farmhouse as Hank and Rolf returned from the tractor path. "What did you come up with?" he asked Hank.

"We found Helen's footprints on the dirt tractor lane that passed by their urban warfare practice area," Hank replied. "Helen's prints ended there, but the tire tracks kept going. None of the tracks appeared to be returning, only going straight ahead. We need to find out where that lane ends up."

"We can check on Google Maps on my laptop," Hanratty said.

Hank and Rolf followed Hanratty to his cruiser where he booted up the computer. He brought up the map of the area and zoomed in on Duesterbeck's farm. "It looks like that tractor lane goes all the way back to Hartman Road. About another half mile past the practice area.

"Let's see if we can make it back there with the Honda," Hank said. "Helen could be back there along that lane!"

Hank gave Rolf the large flashlight he always stowed in Helen's trunk. "I'll go slow, Rolf. You keep an eye out the passenger side." Hank motored at a crawl past the practice area, stopping occasionally to examine open areas more thoroughly with their lights. They called Helen's name and stood quietly to listen but only heard their own breathing. When they came out on the narrow, paved Hartman Road, they repeated the routine for a mile in both directions. No sign of Helen could be found. They returned dejectedly to the farmhouse.

Chapter 12

When Hank and Rolf arrived back at the farmhouse they were met by Hanratty. "We apprehended Carter at his apartment up in Hastings about fifteen minutes ago. I sent Haddix up to watch the apartment and sure enough he tried to sneak in. Probably for some clothes and money. No sign of Helen. They are questioning him as we speak."

"Should we head up there?" Hank asked.

"No, not yet. Let's wait and see what he has to say first. I have to remain here to wait for the ATF unit. They should be arriving within the hour to examine all the weapons in the arsenal. They had to roust a judge out of bed to obtain a search warrant."

"I'venever felt so helpless in my life," Hank said. "It's overwhelming to think about what might have happened to Helen. I feel powerless now that I have to depend on others. When I was working I was in charge of the investigations. Don't get me wrong, Bill, I know you're doing the best you can with the information you have to work with."

"Hank, now you know what's like to be on the other side of the fence. To be family of the victim and having to endure the agonizing wait to hear the report, good or bad, about a missing loved one," Hanratty replied.

Fifteen minutes later Hanratty received word from Trooper Haddix on the questioning of Carter. Hank could overhear a bit of Hanratty's side of the conversation. "I see. What about the blood in the boat? . . . OK, I'll let him know."

Hanratty turned and looked at Hank.

"Good or bad?" Hank asked with a feeling of impending dread.

"Jim claims Carter looked like he was beat up in a brawl," Hanratty replied. "He has a black eye, bent nose, and a few loose front teeth. Carter said your wife did it to him. He said that it's his blood in the boat. Helen managed to knock him out with the chloroform,and when he came to she was gone. He claims that he took off shortly after Duesterbeck arrived."

Hank stood slack-jawed after hearing about Carter's statement. He was smiling when he finally managed to speak. "Carter claims Helen beat him up?"

"That's what he claims," Hanratty said.

"I'll be damned! Well, so far the news is good, but it could also mean that it was Duesterbeck that found her and took her hostage," Hank said. "We've got to find that son-of-a bitch!"

Hanratty's phone rang again and he turned away to answer it. Once again Hank could hear one side of the conversation. Hanratty wasn't much of a talker. Hank heard, "Yes, he is still here . . . Yes, Ed, I will let him know. OK, right away.

When Hanratty ended the call he turned to Hank, "That was Ed Harrison. He was relaying a message from the FBI agents on the scene at the cruise boat. They want you back there immediately for a debriefing."

"Damn," Hank said. "I need to stay out here and keep searching. We are positive Helen was here. I should stay here until you find Duesterbeck. If he doesn't have her that means she is still in the area of the farm."

"Hank, it may take some time to locate Duesterbeck. There isn't much you can do here in the dark. Why don't you and Rolf head back to the *Princess* as requested. It may be wise to stay on the good side of the FBI agents. We may need their help to find Helen."

"I guess you're right, Bill. But I'll be back here as soon as they are through with me. I need to try to make more sense out of the tracks I found."

Hank and Rolf arrived back at the *Lansing Princess* riverboat close to midnight. The parking lot entrance was lined with news vans and the area leading down to the dock was blocked with Lansing Police patrol cars.

Hank motored past the vans and stopped in front of the police barricade. An officer approached his open window. "You'll have to turn around, sir. No one is allowed past this point."

"Officer, I am Hank Moran. Detective Harrison said the FBI wanted to meet with me." Hank showed the officer his ID.

"Stay right here, sir, I'll call the detective."

A moment later the officer returned and moved the barricade. "You are cleared to proceed, sir. They are inside the boat waiting for you."

Hank and Rolf were met by Detective Harrison when they entered the *Lansing Princess*, which had become a makeshift FBI command center. They were introduced to agents Don Kratz and Carl Bishop. Kratz was the lead agent of the Detroit Regional Office.

"Mr. Moran, thanks for getting here so quick," Agent Kratz said. "I know it's been a long night for you, but we need your input to wrap up our preliminary report. We know how you must feel with Mrs. Moran unaccounted for so we will keep this as short as possible."

"Agent Kratz, I assume the FBI is now in charge of the investigation, so I'll ask *you* if any progress has been made in finding Duesterbeck."

"We have all the statewide police forces in Michigan, Indiana, and Ohio on alert for his vehicle, Mr. Moran. The only way for him to leave the state is south into Indiana or Ohio. Fortunately, the lakes hem him in to the east and west. The Canadian authorities have been alerted at all border crossings. All the news stations are continually airing bulletins with his picture and a description of his vehicle. Unfortunately, that's all I have to report right now."

"OK, Agent Kratz, let's get this report over with. I need to get back to the farm and I need to know as soon as you apprehend Duesterbeck. If he isn't holding Helen hostage, I need to widen the search for her in the area of the farm."

"Before we get started, do you have a picture of Mrs. Moran that we could air along with Duesterbeck's?"

"Yes, I have two in my wallet you can use." Hank chose the latest picture he had of Helen and handed it to Agent Kratz.

"It will only take a minute to scan this," Kratz said as he handed it to Agent Bishop. "Carl, email this as extremely urgent to all the networks to air along with Duesterbeck's picture."

Hank and Rolf were debriefed together, with Hank starting with the murder of Agusto Soto in Indiana, Wengert's fake hit-and-run, and the rescue of the senator. Rolf filled them in on the now known involvement of the CCB and Walter Duesterbeck in the attempted murder of thesenator.

When the report was complete, Hank said, "I got so caught up in my wife's disappearance that I failed to ask how the senator is doing. I don't see him or Clarice here on the boat."

"Senator Westbrook is doing just fine," Kratz said. "His wife insisted that he go to the hospital to have his head examined because of the blow he received. He didn't want to go, saying he took harder hits as a linebacker in college, but his wife reminded him that college was thirty years ago and he is no longer a young stud. He finally gave in and went to the ER."

"I know about the senator's college career," Hank said. "As a matter of fact, five years ago he made a flying tackle of a suspected bank robber down in Louisiana and saved my life."

"Well, Mr. Moran, it looks like you returned the favor. The State of Michigan still has a great senator, thanks to you."

"I hope it is only a small minority that is disappointed in my rescue attempt. The senator did receive a little negative feedback from the citizenry this evening."

"A politician can never please everyone, Mr. Moran. By the way, an old friend of yours from the Knoxville office sends his greetings. He heard about your exploits on the national news."

"You must be referring to Agent Emory."

"None other. Agent Emory requested that you give him a call at your earliest convenience. He said he has an update on their effort to locate the preacher. The way he talked you were instrumental in solving the murders of those men last month. He had only good things to say about you."

"I really want to hear what he has to say about the preacher," Hank said. "I'll be sure to give him a call when this situation is over up here. Right now I need to get back out to Duesterbeck's farm. Oh, Agent Kratz, can I have one of your cards in case I need to contact you?"

"Here you go, Mr. Moran. I wrote my cell number on the bottom. And here is your wife's purse. I am sure she will be needing it when you find her."

"Thanks, Agent Kratz. I'll see that she gets it." Hank reached in his pocket, withdrew Helen's T.C.B. bracelet, and placed it in the purse.

"Hank, can you drop me off at the *Journal* before you head back to the farm?" Rolf asked. "I need to beat the deadline for the morning paper. I have quite a story to write."

"No problem, Rolf, let's go."

On the way back to the farm, Hank pulled into an all-night gas station to fill up the Honda and buy some additional batteries for his flashlight. Fox News was playing on the TV behind the counter. When Hank signed the charge slip, the clerk asked to see his ID. When the clerk saw his name, he scratched his head and then said, "Mr. Hank Moran. I know I just heard that name on the news. Are you the guy that rescued the senator?"

"Yes, that was me," Hank said.

"Damn, you shoulda let him drown," the clerk responded.

More negative feedback, Hank thought as he walked back to the Honda shaking his head. *Apparently the senator's proposed legislation isn't very popular.*

It was two thirty AM when Hank arrived back at Duesterbeck's farm. He was met by Trooper Hanratty when he reached the farmhouse. Hank anticipated he would still be onsite and presented Hanratty with a large cup of coffee he had purchased at the gas station.

"Hope you like it black, Bill." Hank said.

"Black is fine. Right now I'll take anything I can get," Hanratty answered."

"Anything happen while I was gone?"

"No, it's been fairly quiet. The ATF boys are still in the barn. They found a cache of automatic weapons that haven't been registered."

"Doesn't surprise me," Hank said. "Boys will be boys."

"What's *your* next step, Hank?"

"If you don't mind, I want to head back out to the urban warfare practice area to get a better feel for the tracks I saw. Right now it's the only thing I have to go on."

"You're free to go ahead, Hank. It's best if you keep busy while we wait on news about Duesterbeck. So far we haven't found a trace of him."

"If you hear anything while I'm out there give me a call."

Hanratty wrote down the number Hank gave him. He had left his cell phone back at the motorhome, but luckily Helen had brought hers along in her purse, which was now on the front seat of the Honda. Hank retrieved the cell phone and started walking.

Hank walked the quarter mile back along the tractor lane to the group of false front buildings. The area reminded him of a set for a Wild West movie. All that was missing was the saloon sign above one of the open doorways.

He once again located Helen's shoeprints leading into one of the building fronts. He also noticed larger shoeprints, about size twelve, leading in the same direction as Helen's. No prints were visible on the hard packed gravel behind the building facade. He searched, but he found only the larger men's prints heading in the opposite direction back to the tractor lane. None of Helen's. Hank's spirits were immediately lifted as he thought of the possibility that Duesterbeck hadn't found her after all.

Hank immediately broadened his search to include the tall grassy area behind the gravel that edged on a cornfield.Next to the cornfield he found a trail through the grass. The trail looked fresh as the grass was still flattened from numerous footprints. He was about to follow the trail when he heard a vehicle approaching on the tractor lane from the opposite direction of the farmhouse.

Hank ran and hid behind one of the building facades. The vehicle had no headlights on as it slowly approached the practice area and then came to a halt thirty yards in front of him. The half moon was now high in the night sky and afforded enough light to assure Hank that the vehicle was a black Escalade.

Hank watched through one of the paneless windows as a man exited the vehicle wearing what appeared to be night vision goggles. No interior lights came on in the vehicle. The man tucked a handgun in his belt, then reached into the vehicle and came out with what appeared to be an assault rifle. He quietly closed the door to the Escalade.

Hank ducked just as the man turned in his direction. Hank knew some goggles had thermal imaging capabilities and hoped his heat signature wasn't visible behind the facade. He counted to fifteen and risked another look out the window. He saw Duesterbeck had turned and was walking back the tractor lane towards the farmhouse.

Hank's only thought was to warn Trooper Hanratty. Being unarmed himself there was nothing else he could do. He had given Hanratty his number but didn't think to get Hanratty's. Then he remembered Agent Kratz's card in his pocket. With the aid of his flashlight he read Kratz's number and punched it into Helen's cell phone.

It took five long, agonizing rings before Kratz answered. "Agent Kratz, FBI."

"Agent Kratz, Hank Moran. I am out at Duesterbeck's farm a quarter mile from the farmhouse. Duesterbeck just showed up fully armed and wearing night vision goggles. You need to warn Trooper Hanratty as quick as you can. Duesterbeck is heading to the farmhouse from the rear side of the barn."

"Hank, how did you—"

Hank cut him off, "Agent Kratz, there is no time to talk! Warn Hanratty, NOW!"

"OK, Hank, I'm on it."

Hank ended the call and peered out the window again. Duesterbeck was nowhere in sight. He stood up and peeked around the doorway. No Duesterbeck. He ran to the Escalade and ducked behind it. The engine was still warm and would mask his heat signature if Duesterbeck happened to look back.

Hank crept along the side of the Escalade and searched the interior with his light. He made sure to shade the light with his left hand to make it harder for Duesterbeck to spot it.

Hank had mixed feelings about not finding Helen in the big SUV. It could mean Helen was still on foot in the area or, he feared, Duesterbeck could have dropped her anywhere in the county. He had no choice but to question Duesterbeck.

Two minutes later Helen's cell phone warbled. Hank answered it quickly. "Hank Moran," he answered in a near whisper.

"Hank, Bill Hanratty. Thanks for the heads up on Duesterbeck."

"Be careful, Bill. He's fully armed with a handgun and assault rifle and heading your way. Try to stay invisible. He's wearing night vision."

"He's not holding your wife by any chance is he?"

"No, Helen was not with him. Do your best to take him alive. We need to question him."

"I'll do my best, Hank. I just hope he's not planning suicide by cop."

There was a slight pause then Hanratty said. "Gotta go, Hank. One of the ATF boys just motioned that they spotted him approaching."

Three Hours Earlier

When Helen saw the light approaching, she immediately turned into the cornfield, stepped through the stalks, and penetrated the field ten rows deep. A few minutes later she saw faint traces of a light beam penetrating the corn and froze. She thought it best to stand rigidly still rather than duck down. Her pursuer might see the movement.

Helen heard Duesterbeck make an utterance about leaving, and not knowing if it was a ploy, thought it better to stay put until she was sure he was gone. Five minutes later she heard a car door shut and an engine start. The sound of the motor faded into the distance. "I agree with you, Mr. Duesterbeck. Time to vacate the premises," Helen whispered to herself.

Helen quickly backtracked out of the corn and proceeded along the edge of the field.She reached the end of the cornfield and came upon a no trespassing sign fastened to a post of a barbed wire fence which apparently marked the end of Duesterbeck's property. After weighing her options, she decided to go through the fence thinking that a neighboring farmhouse with a telephone should be nearby.

She found an area of the fence where the ground dipped slightly, affording a larger gap between the bottom strand of barbed wire and the ground. While lying on her back parallel to the fence she lifted the strand up and wriggled sideways until she was clear on the other side.

The grassy field ahead had a gradual incline to the horizon a quarter mile ahead. Helen wrapped her now soiled sweater tighter around her as she could feel the night air turning cooler. Fatigue started to set in as she neared the top of the rise.

From her view on top of the hill she could make out the shape of a house and farm buildings in the valley below. *I hope they aren't CCB members,* she silently prayed as she started down the hill.

As she neared the farmhouse a large mixed breed dog suddenly appeared at her side and emitted a low throaty growl. Helen froze and began talking sweetly in a high feminine southern voice to the dog, trying not to let on she was shaking with fright. Her nonthreatening tone had the desired calming effect as the dog moved closer and nudged her hand. "Some guard dog you are," Helen said as she liberally scratched the big mutt's neck.

The dog responded gratefully by leaning against Helen, wanting more. Helen willingly obliged, feeling relieved to be able to cement the relationship. The dog followed her up onto the porch of the farmhouse and sat dutifully by her side as she knocked on the door. Receiving no answer, she knocked again. Again, no answer from inside.

"I don't know about you, big dog, but I'm awfully tired and cold. Do you mind if I check out the barn?"

The dog replied by nudging Helen's hand again. "OK, so that's the deal. I scratch your neck, and then I can check out the barn?"

Helen entered the upper level of the barn, which was stacked with bales of sweet smelling hay. In near total darkness she found her way to the hay bales. She was careful to avoid the hay hole, a feature she knew was in most barns, used to drop hay to the lower floor for cattle feed. She could hear the cattle one floor below.

Feeling sure someone would be around in the morning to feed and milk the cows, she crawled up two levels of hay bales and, feeling the latent heat in the hay, curled up and fell sound asleep.

Previously, when Duesterbeck heard the distant police siren he gave up his search for the Moran woman and headed back to his SUV. Sitting in his Escalade he considered all his options. He had to find a safe hideout. He had friends in another battalion to the north above Cadillac who would hide him for a while, but he reasoned his chances of making it there without being caught were nil.

As he approached the end of the tractor lane near Hartman Road he decided to back into a side lane then pull to the side behind a dense copse of raspberry bushes. "No place like home!" he said aloud to himself. "I'll just sit it out here for a while and see what happens. I think my ass is grass no matter what I do. If I'm going down, it will be on my own terms and on my own land!"

Close to an hour after he parked he saw the headlights of a car approaching slowly down the tractor lane. He could see flashlight beams shining out both sides of the car and someone called the name "Helen." The car stopped briefly at the side lane and a light was shined in his direction. He was sure he wasn't spotted as the car then continued onto Hartman Road. Twenty minutes later he heard the car return and continue back towards his farmhouse.

Duesterbeck remained parked in the same spot, occasionally nodding off. The third time he reopened his eyes the clock on the dash read 3:00 AM. "I'll be damned if

I'm going to sit here till daylight and have them find me asleep in my car," he said to himself.

He dimmed all the dash lights and donned the night vision goggles that were laying on the backseat. With the goggles fitted and adjusted, he started the Escalade and slowly made his way to the tractor lane. He decided to motor halfway back then approach the farmhouse on foot.

Chapter 13

Present Time

As soon as Hanratty ended the call that announced Duesterbeck's approach to the farmhouse, Hank decided to search Duesterbeck's SUV in the hope of finding another weapon. He opened the passenger side door and checked the glove compartment. Nothing there but an owner's manual and old auto service receipts. The center console proved more fruitful. Under a small but fully packed moneybag, his light revealed a familiar type handgun. It was a .38 police special revolver. The revolver was identical to the one issued to him over thirty years ago when he graduated from the police academy. Hank opened the cylinder and found it to be fully loaded with six cartridges. No additional ammo was in the console.

Hank's next step was to disable the SUV to prevent Duesterbeck's escape should events go in the fugitive's favor. Hank found a small, pointed piece of gravel, unscrewed the tire valve cap on the left-rear tire and let the air out. He did likewise for the tire on the right rear.

With the SUV disabled to Hank's satisfaction, he was about to call Hanratty when he heard gunfire coming from the direction of the farmhouse.

Trooper Hanratty and the two ATF agents watched as Duesterbeck approached on the tractor lane. They realized Duesterbeck's night vision goggles did not have advanced thermal imaging or else they surely would have been spotted in their positions on either side of the barn.

Hanratty allowed Duesterbeck to approach to within ninety feet of the barn then shouted, "Walter Duesterbeck, throw down your weapons and put your hands behind your head."

Duesterbeck's immediate reaction was to level his assault rifle in the direction of Hanratty's voice and fire a burst of rounds. He then ran to his right and hid behind an ancient manure spreader just beyond the outer stone wall of the barnyard. Duesterbeck's firing splintered the corner of the barn Hanratty was positioned behind. He had ducked back just in time when he saw Duesterbeck leveling the weapon.

The return fire by Hanratty and the two ATF agents was aimed where Duesterbeck was before he ran to the right. No further firing by Duesterbeck concealed his new position.

Hanratty, in phone contact with the two ATF agents, called "One of you fire to the left and one to the right of his previous position. If he returns fire, I'll watch to see if I can locate his position."

The agents directed three rounds each as requested. The rounds to the left drew immediate return fire by Duesterbeck. Hanratty spotted his position and fired two rounds that ricocheted off the old steel manure spreader.

When Hank heard the gunfire coming from the direction of the farmhouse he immediately headed on foot in that direction. A hundred and fifty feet up the tractor lane he saw an object lying on the side of the lane. The moon's light reflected on a lens of the night vision goggles Duesterbeck had been wearing.

Hank picked up the goggles and tried them on. He flipped the on switch and nothing happened—the batteries were dead. Hank immediately called Hanratty.

Hanratty looked at the incoming number and answered on the first ring. "Hank, is that you?"

"Bill, I heard gunfire and headed in your direction. I found Duesterbeck's headgear. The batteries ran out on him."

"That's good to hear. At least we're on a level playing field now."

"What's his present position?"

"His last return fire came from behind a piece of machinery at the bottom of the barnyard. It would be to your right if you're facing the barn."

"Keep him busy, Bill. I'll coming up the tractor lane. Leave our call connected. I'll let you know when I'm ready to cut in behind him and you'll need to cease fire. I don't want to catch a stray round."

"Hank, are you armed?"

"Of course I am. Did you think I would try to do this with rocks and sticks? Duesterbeck had a spare revolver in his console. By the way, I also disabled his SUV."

"Good work, Hank, I guess there's no talking you out of this. Besides, we seem to be out-gunned."

"Hang in there, I'm on my way. And don't forget, leave our call connected. Now start shooting and keep him pinned down."

The shooting resumed as Hank approached on the tractor lane. There was an occasional round returned by Duesterbeck. He was obviously trying to save ammunition.

Hank saw a deteriorated fence that once held a gate that closed off the tractor path to contain livestock in the barnyard area. The fence row ran parallel to the stone wall sixty feet behind Duesterbeck's position.

Hank whispered into his phone, "Bill, can you hear me?"

"Affirmative, Hank."

"OK, hold your fire. I am going to cut in behind him along an old fence line. It looks like the grass is tall enough around the fence to give me cover."

"Hank, be careful.Don't take any chances. Take him out if you have to."

"I know the procedure, Bill."

Hank crouched low and cut diagonally behind the fence to a position he was sure was directly in line with Duesterbeck. He then lay down in a prone position on his elbows with the revolver out in front. He slowly parted the grass and saw Duesterbeck sitting, facing in his direction, with his back against the wheel of an ancient manure spreader.

Hank reached under himself and removed the golf ball sized rock that was irritating his hip bone. He smiled as he realized the irony of his intended diversion. Hank lobbed the rock and it struck the stone wall thirty feet to the right of Duesterbeck.

Duesterbeck's immediate reaction was to fall on his belly in the direction of the noise and let loose with a five round burst. Hank now had him in the position he wanted him.

"It's over Duesterbeck! Put down your weapon!" Hank demanded.

Duesterbeck wanted no part of surrender and started his turn to aim the assault rifle in Hank's direction. Hank knew that if he hesitated he would be cut down by Duesterbeck's automatic rifle. He halted Duesterbeck's motion with an accurately placed round into the fugitive's right forearm and the stock of the assault rifle. Duesterbeck recoiled his right arm and started to reach for the assault rifle with his left hand. Hank fired again and the dirt erupted in front of Duesterbeck's outstretched hand. Duesterbeck cradled his injured right arm with his left hand and sat upright against the iron wheel.

"Be a good boy now, Walter. Stay where you are and don't move," Hank shouted.

Hank retrieved the cell phone from his hip pocket. "You still on, Bill?"

"I hear you, Hank. Are you OK?"

"I'm fine. Duesterbeck is down. If you approach him from your right side I'll keep him covered."

Hank saw Hanratty and one ATF agent approach Duesterbeck as suggested. The other agent appeared directly above the wall. Hanratty kicked the assault rifle out of Duesterbeck's reach while the ATF agent relieved him of the handgun that was tucked into the back of his belt.

Seeing that the situation was controlled, Hank slid under the fence and joined the group. Duesterbeck glared at Hank and Hank had only one question for him.

"Duesterbeck, what did you do with my wife?"

Duesterbeck, falling into a state of shock from the arm wound, was confused. "Wife? I don't know what you are talking about."

"You and your cohorts kidnapped my wife off the *Lansing Princess*. We found evidence that she was here on your farm."

"Moran, you bastard.You screwed up all our plans."

"Sorry about that, Walter. But as I heard you say once before, 'Life has its twists and turns.' Now, we are going to let you lie there and bleed until you tell me where she is."

"I have no idea where she is, Moran. She escaped from Carter before I got out here. I tried to track her down but I had to give up when I heard the police sirens. That must be one hell of a woman you got there, doing in Carter like that."

"That she is," Hank replied. "Bill, I'm going back out to the urban warfare compound. I started to pick up a trail when Duesterbeck arrived on the scene. If you don't mind I'm going to hang on to this revolver awhile longer."

"Go ahead, Hank. I don't think Mr. Duesterbeck will have any further use for it, but I'll need it back as evidence."

Hank trotted the quarter mile back to the compound and immediately turned to follow the tracks he found earlier in the grass that ran parallel with the edge of the cornfield. He eventually reached a spot where the multiple impressions from foot traffic turned into what appeared to be the track of a lone individual.

Hank shined the light around and spotted Helen's footprints entering and leaving the cornfield. *She must have hidden in the cornfield and then continued on after Duesterbeck gave up the search,* Hank surmised.

He followed the single set of tracks that eventually reached a barbed wire fence at the end of the cornfield. He found an impression in the grass where someone had slid under the barbed wire so he did the same.

The grass in the adjoining field was shorter and made the trail harder to follow. However, he succeeded in following the faint trail to the top of the rise where he saw a farmhouse and barn one quarter mile below. Hank's instincts and the trail led him in that direction. He picked up the pace as he headed down the hill.

It was 4:00 AM as Hank approached the farmhouse. He was opening the gate to the yard when a large dog appeared and issued a deep throated growl and bark. An elderly man appeared on the front porch and leveled a double barreled shotgun in Hank's direction.

"Hold it right there, fella," the man said. Why are you sneaking around on my land at four in the morning?"

143

"I'm looking for my wife," Hank replied. I tracked her here from over at Duesterbeck's place."

"Man that can't keep track of his wife ain't no concern of mine. Now turn around and go back where you came from."

"You don't understand, sir. She was kidnapped by Duesterbeck and escaped. I followed her trail to your place."

"Well, I ain't seen her. Course she might have been here earlier when I was in bed. Can't hear a damn thing without my hearing aid in."

Hank noticed the big dog sniffing out a trail in the direction of the barn.

"Sir, do you mind if I look in your barn before I leave?"

"Hold on a minute. I'll go with you. Have to start the milkin anyway. We'll take a quick look, and then you gotta leave."

The old man reached inside his doorway and brought out an old kerosene lantern. As the two were walking towards the barn Hank said, "I haven't introduced myself. I'm Hank Moran from Kenner, Louisiana."

"Welcome to Michigan, Mr. Moran. My name is Henry Becker. Most people call me Hank also. Tell me, how did your wife happen to be kidnapped?"

"We were on the *Lansing Princess* riverboat last night at the invitation of Senator Westbrook. Your neighbor, Walter Duesterbeck, tried to murder the senator and I wound up saving him from drowning in the river. While I was in the river with the senator Duesterbeck kidnapped my wife and brought her out here."

"I always thought that guy had a few screws loose."

Hank grinned and asked, "Who, the senator?"

"No, the senator's fine. I meant my crazy neighbor. I've been complainin to the sheriff for years about those idiots next door," Becker replied. "Sometimes it sounded like a war was goin on over there."

As they approached the upper level barn door the dog stood in front of the door and issued a low 'ruff.' Henry Becker opened the door and the dog went charging in. When Hank and Henry Becker entered the barn they could see that the dog had jumped up onto the second layer of hay bales and was nudging the hand of a sleeping Helen Moran.

"Well, I'll be," Henry Becker uttered.

Hank rushed to Helen's side and shouted "Helen . . . Helen," as he tried to shake her awake. Hank knew that Helen was a sound sleeper and waited patiently as she stirred and awakened from her deep slumber.

Helen opened her eyes and saw Hank looking down at her in the dim light cast by the kerosene lamp. "Oh, Hank, you're OK! I was worried sick about you," she said as she reached up and took his hands. Hank pulled her up and into his arms.

"Are you hurt or injured?" Hank asked in a state of high anxiety. "I thought I lost you."

"I'm OK, Hank. I seem to have lost my bracelet though and ruined my outfit."

"I found your bracelet stuck to some duct tape in the bottom of Carter's boat. It's safe and sound in your purse."

"Hmff, I'll let you two lovers get reacquainted," Henry Becker said. "If you can wait two hours till I finish my milkin I'll give you a ride to wherever your car is."

"Thanks for the offer, Mr. Becker, but I'll call Trooper Hanratty over at the Duesterbecks' and have him come and pick us up," Hank replied.

Hanratty was just finishing up at the Duesterbecks' when Hank called. He was elated that Hank had found Helen uninjured and said he'd be right over to pick them up.

Hank and Helen left the barn and walked the short distance to the farmhouse to wait for Hanratty. The dog would not leave Helen's side in anticipation of more friendly scratches on his neck.

"Looks like you acquired a new friend while you were here," Hank said.

"Yeah he's a typical male," Helen said. "A little scratch here and there and you can't get rid of him."

"Helen, there's a sore spot right between my shoulder blades. I think I might have pulled a muscle in the river last night."

"You'll get your turn when we get back to the RV park, big boy."

Hanratty pulled up at Becker's farmhouse five minutes later and Hank and Helen climbed into the backseat. "How is Duesterbeck?" Hank asked as Hanratty turned his cruiser around and headed back out to the road.

"Your bullet tore up his right arm pretty bad but the EMTs think he should have no problem pulling through. He is presently in the ER up in Hastings."

"Did I just hear you say that Hank shot Duesterbeck?" Helen exclaimed.

"Yes he did, Mrs. Moran. He defused a very difficult and dangerous situation by doing so."

"Oh, Hank. You only ever shot one other person in your whole thirty two years on the force. Are you OK?"

"Helen, I feel fine about shooting Duesterbeck. It was either him or me. What I don't feel fine about is I might have been able to save Griggs in the river, but I didn't try."

"What happened in the river, Hank?"

"I'll tell you about it later after we get back to the Bounder."

"I am afraid you won't be able to leave right away, Hank. Your FBI friends showed up just before I came to pick you up. They want to get a statement from you and Helen before you leave. And a News Center 6 van pulled in right behind them."

Hank groaned and said to Helen, "Looks like our long night just got a little longer."

Agent Kratz decided to use the arsenal room in the barn for the interview with the Morans so as to avoid disturbing Mrs. Duesterbeck as much as possible. He realized that all the activity—gunfire and the shooting of her son—was a great strain on the elderly lady.

Helen listened intently as Hank related the actions that took place, beginning with his arrival back at the farm, the arrival of Duesterbeck, Hank's wounding of Duesterbeck, and his search for and finding of Helen.

Helen related her story, and Hank looked on in awe and admiration as she told of faking unconsciousness when being abducted from the cruise boat, the ride in the tarp covered boat where she freed herself of the duct tape, and her dynamic take down of Carter.

When she was through Agent Kratz said, "Mrs. Moran, you are a very resourceful woman."

"Sometimes a woman just has to take care of business," Helen replied.

"Well, you sure did, Mrs. Moran. I think that's all I need from you two at this time," Agent Kratz said. "I'll be in touch if we have any further questions."

On the walk back to the Honda the Morans were set upon by the TV news crew. A microphone was shoved into Hank's face, and a female news reporter asked him what it felt like to be a hero.

Hank pushed the microphone aside and said, "We are sorry, but we are both very tired and there will be no TV interviews. Our only interview will be conducted by Rolf Kramden of the *State Journal*. You can read all about it in the paper."

Hank and Helen ignored the protests and quickly retreated to the Honda.

The sun was starting to peek over the horizon when they arrived back at the RV park. Helen's first order of business was a hot shower and a warm bed. Hank followed suit, and when he crawled in bed beside Helen she was already sound asleep.

Chapter 14

Hank was awakened from a fitful sleep by the chiming of his cell phone. He saw the time on the dresser clock was eleven forty five am.

"This is Hank," he said when he hit the answer button on his phone.

"Hank, Rolf Kramden. I have some news on the blood from the board you found. It's Wengert's! Also they found a large crowbar in Griggs's truck bed with blood on it. It looks like your intuitive powers were right again."

"Well, I'm glad he left that crowbar in the bed of his truck instead of taking it along on the boat. He could have used that on me and the senator instead of a clumsy oar."

"Yeah, you kind of lucked out there."

"Now that they are positive it was Wengert's blood on the board I wonder how this is all going to work out as far as Sheriff Engle is concerned."

"Hanratty and his boss are discussing how to handle the sheriff as we speak. They think the only way to make any charges stick on him is to have either Carter or Jacobs rat on him and state that he tried to cover up the murder as a hit-and-run. Duesterbeck refuses to talk at all."

"Rolf, wasn't Carter with Griggs and Wengert when they went deer spotting the night Wengert was killed?"

"That's right he was."

"I don't think it would be to Carter's advantage to turn on the sheriff. He could always claim Griggs committed the murder and he didn't know anything about it."

"Yeah, you're right, Hank. What about Jacobs? Do you think he would testify against Engle?"

"Jacobs is facing a very serious charge in the attempted murder of Senator Westbrook. I don't think the D.A. would want to give up anything to entice Jacobs to implicate the sheriff in an unrelated case. Of course we know the cases are related in a roundabout way, however, in legal terms they aren't."

"Well, Hank, Engle is up for reelection in a few months. I can always try him in the court of public opinion and attempt to screw that up for him. Looks like I've got another story to write."

"Glad you mentioned that, Rolf. I told the TV news reporter last night that Helen and I would give our only interviews to you. You have a *few* more stories to write."

"In that case, I'll be right over. I'll bring a pizza and the beer."

"Make it the works with double cheese and ice brewed beer. We haven't had anything to eat since last evening's dinner cruise."

Rolf appeared at the campground one hour later with beer and pizza in hand. After a brief lunch the interviews began.

Hank had not yet told Helen about all that happened in his rescue of Senator Westbrook. She listened intently as he described all that took place in the water when Griggs tried to drown them. He again related how he felt regretful about not attempting to pull Griggs out of the river.

When hearing Hank's story Helen said, "Hank, I forbid you to feel bad about your actions concerning Griggs. You did a wonderful and brave thing in jumping into that river to rescue the senator. You had no way of knowing what condition Griggs was in when you knocked him out of his boat. He could have as easily drowned you if you tried to rescue him. As far as I am concerned he didn't deserve rescuing. He fully deserved what he got. And I do not feel anything but tremendously happy about having my great husband alive and by my side."

"Helen's right, Hank," Rolf added. "Look at it as a simple case of self defense. Besides, we don't know as yet what caused Griggs's death."

It was then Helen's turn to tell her story to Rolf. Rolf seemed totally amazed at Helen's parts of the story where she feigned unconsciousness and her slam-bang escape from Carter.

When she completed her story Rolf said, "Holy cow, Mrs. Moran, that sounded like something you see only in the movies."

"She is a wonderful and resourceful woman," Hank said. "And I feel honored to be married to her."

"OK, that's enough you two," Helen said. "Let's finish this pizza so Hank can take me shopping. I ruined a perfectly good outfit last night and it needs to be replaced if we are going to continue on our journey."

"Yes,ma'am," Hank and Rolf said in unison.

Hank sat in a husband chair inside the Towne Center Mall Talbots store as Helen made multiple appearances in new outfits. She valued his opinion as she always said he was the one who has to look at her—that and the fact he was footing the bill. He had just given his approval on a pair of black slacks and a turquoise and black paisley cardigan sweater over a white collared shirt when his cell phone rang.

"This is Hank Moran."

"Hank, Senator Westbrook. I heard the good news about Helen. I just wanted to call and tell you how much Clarice and I appreciate what you've done and invite you both for dinner this evening."

"Senator, you're not talking about another riverboat cruise are you?"

"Good Lord, no! I have had my fill of riverboats for a long time. Besides, Clarice wouldn't even let me get near one. We would like you to come over to our place for just a nice quiet get together."

"Sounds good, Senator. I'll let Helen know when she comes out of the dressing room. She ruined a good outfit when she was kidnapped last night and we're at the Talbots store shopping for a new one."

"OK, Hank, let's make it for seven. I'll email directions to your phone."

"Thanks, Senator, see you then."

Hank had just ended the call when Helen reappeared with her new wardrobe selections including a pair of basic black pumps. The shoes she bought the previous day were ruined in her trek through the farm pastures and cornfield.

"Helen, while you were changing, Senator Westbrook called and invited us for dinner at his house tonight. I hope you don't mind that I accepted the invitation."

"As long as it's not another riverboat cruise it's OK with me."

"I made sure of that before I accepted," Hank answered with a chuckle.

"OK, I'm done. Let's go to checkout."

When Hank presented his credit card to the clerk she saw the name and handed it back to him.

"Your card won't be necessary, Mr. Moran. Mrs. Westbrook called and said to put all your purchases on her account."

Hank started to protest but the clerk related that Mrs. Westbrook said not to let the Morans pay by any means whatsoever.

As they were leaving the store Helen jokingly said, "Darn, I should have added that other outfit to the pile."

As they arrived back at their Bounder motorhome, Hank remembered that their reservation was up and they were scheduled to leave in the morning. "Helen, do you realize we have to vacate the premises in the morning?"

"If you are thinking about extending our stay again forget it," Helen replied. "I've seen enough of the Michigan countryside to last a lifetime. I'm ready to move on."

"And so we shall!" Hank agreeably answered.

After Helen removed the tags from her new outfit she decided to take a short snooze to catch up on her sleep before dinner with the Westbrooks.

Remembering that Agent Chris Emory from Knoxville had requested that Hank give him a call, he settled into his recliner and hit the phone book entry for the agent.

Emory was the lead agent in the Knoxville regional FBI office and had worked with Hank in the solving of the Leviticus murders the previous month. Agent Emory answered on the third ring.

"Agent Chris Emory."

"Chris, Hank Moran. I got word from Agent Kratz over here in Michigan that you wanted me to call you."

"Yes I did, Hank. I thought you might be interested to know that your hunch about the whereabouts of the preacher panned out."

"That's great, Chris, tell me about it."

"We located an old resume of his, as you suggested, and found that he performed volunteer work in Guayaquil, Ecuador after his graduation from seminary school. We contacted the Guayaquil Police and sent them his picture, which they were then kind enough to publish in the local papers. A merchant from a small town in the nearby mountains was visiting relatives in Guayaquil and saw the picture. He recognized Brantley as his new neighbor who was renting a room in the house next door to his shop. Brantley is now in custody in Guayaquil awaiting extradition. I'm flying down there next week with a US marshal to bring him back."

"That's really good news, Chris. I can't wait to tell Helen."

"How are you and Helen doing after your latest escapade in Michigan?"

"We're both fine. No the worse for wear. Helen is napping right now. She wanted to rest up for tonight's dinner at Senator Westbrook's. We'll be leaving in the morning to head east."

"How is the senator? I heard that you returned the favor for his flying tackle down in Kenner five years ago."

"Last time I saw him he was a little waterlogged, but he is doing fine."

"Oh, Hank, before I forget, will you be passing by Knoxville any time soon?"

"We are planning to head straight through Ohio to Pennsylvania Amish country. We'll probably pass through Knoxville on our way home."

"Good, let me know a day or two ahead of time. Whitehead's trial is coming up soon and we need you both to stop by and give a deposition. I'm sure we can avoid having to have you testify at his trial."

"We'll be glad to, Chris."

"OK, Hank, I'll be waiting for your call. Give my regards to Helen and keep out of trouble for the remainder of your trip."

"We'll do our best, Chris. I'll call you later."

Hank followed his GPS unit's instructions to the senator's address in a posh neighborhood in East Lansing near the Michigan State University campus.

"Wow! So this is how the one percent lives," exclaimed Helen.

"It looks like the senator isn't doing too bad," Hank commented.

They pulled into the circular drive of a massive colonial style home that looked like it should have been on the front cover of *Architectural Digest*.

They were greeted at the front door by a manservant who showed them the way to the drawing room to the right of the foyer. Senator Kenton Westbrook and his wife, Clarice, arose from their chairs to greet their honored guests.

"Welcome to our home," Clarice said warmly, and gave Hank and Helen each a hug.

Senator Westbrook gave Helen a hug, and surprised Hank with one. "Dinner will be ready shortly," Westbrook said. "While we wait, I want you to try some fantastic brandy I picked up on my last trip to Europe."

As if on cue a waiter appeared with a silver tray holding four cordial glasses.

Clarice told Helen she looked lovely, and trying not to be condescending, asked if it was the new outfit she was wearing. Helen said it was and thanked Clarice for her generosity.

"Helen, there is no need to thank me. It's the very least I could do to repay you for all the trouble you went through for Kenton. I just felt terrible about your ordeal. And to hear about how you outwitted those assholes and defended yourself just made me proud to be able to call you my friend. You are an example of the womanhood that made this country great."

Helen didn't quite know what to say in return and was saved by the announcement that dinner would be served in five minutes.

The Morans were treated like visiting royalty for the evening by their hosts and three seemingly overattentive servants. It seemed that the hired help was glad the senator was still among the living—unlike some of the people Hank met the night before who seemed disappointed that he hadn't left Westbrook to his own fate in the Grand River.

They were served a delicious dinner of blackened rib eye etouffee with a side dish of shrimp stuffed bell peppers.

Helen tasted the stuffed bell peppers and remarked, "I need to talk to your cook about these peppers!"

"I'm sorry, is something wrong with them?" Clarice asked.

"Oh no, quite the contrary.They are delicious," Helen replied.

Five minutes later a small elderly lady appeared at Helen's side and said, "Mrs. Moran, I am Mrs. Kate Berteau, the Westbrook's cook. I need to apologize that I couldn't locate crawfish on such short notice for the stuffed peppers. Being born in Louisiana I know crawfish are normally used."

"There is no need to apologize, Mrs. Berteau. I make the same dish with shrimp myself. Your stuffed peppers taste just like the ones my grandmother made that I could never quite duplicate. Would you be willing to give me your recipe?"

"I will be more than happy to write it down for you, Mrs. Moran," Mrs. Berteau said as she returned to the kitchen.

As dinner was drawing to a close Senator Westbrook said he had an announcement to make. "Hank and Helen, if you didn't already know, I am good friends with the president. I talked with him today and told him about Hank saving my life and about Helen's kidnapping ordeal. He wants to meet you both and has invited the four of us for dinner at the White House. He said he just needs to know a week in advance what evening you will be available and he will make room in his schedule, barring any national emergency."

Hank and Helen were momentarily speechless then Helen spoke. "You may tell the president we will gladly accept his invitation." She then turned to Hank and said, "We'll have to make another stop at a Talbots store."

Clarice laughed and said, "Go girl."

The Westbrooks had to catch an early flight back to Washington, and the Morans had to prep their motorhome for departure in the morning, so they bid goodnight to their hosts at ten.

As the Morans were leaving, Mrs. Berteau presented Helen with an envelope. "Mrs. Moran, here is my recipe for the stuffed peppers. I hope you can read it as my handwriting isn't as steady as it used to be. If you have trouble reading it and can't make out the secret ingredient, my phone number is at the bottom."

Helen thanked her and gave her a hug.

The next morning Hank arose early and walked to the campground office for the morning paper. He was surprised to see Rolf Kramden's interview with Hank and Helen on the front page. The column header for Helen's story read: "Taking care of business."

After a light breakfast, with the Bounder prepped for travel and the Honda hooked up with its tow bar, the Morans were once again on the road.They left the Cottonwood Campground and headed south towards Interstate 80. They would then stay on I-80 all the way into eastern Pennsylvania.

In late afternoon, as they were halfway across Ohio, Hank's cell phone rang. Helen picked it up and saw it was Rolf Kramden calling.

"Hello, Rolf," she said as she clicked on the speaker phone.

"Hello, Helen, I've got some news for Hank. Is he there?"

"I'm right here," Hank replied.

"Hank, I just got word on the medical examiner's report on Griggs. He claims Griggs actually died of a heart attack and didn't drown as you thought. The blow to the chest could have triggered it, but he was doomed for an attack in the very near future considering the condition of his arteries."

"Well, Rolf, that news really helps. I feel much better now," Hank replied.

When the call from Rolf was ended Hank said, "We've got to stop getting involved in these dangerous situations."

"Don't worry, big guy," Helen replied, "How much trouble could we get into in Amish country? And besides, in about two weeks we'll be surrounded by Secret Service."

About the Author

L.D. Knorr was born and raised on a dairy farm in Berks County Pennsylvania and now resides in rural Alabama. His profession as a mechanical engineer required his relocation from Pennsylvania to Mississippi, Texas, and Alabama. He honed his writing skills on engineering related technical papers and reports. Now being retired he is focusing his attention on fiction.

He travels in his RV trailer with his wife Emily to visit family in Pennsylvania and Mississippi. They have been married forty-nine years and were blessed with three talented and creative children.

www.ingramcontent.com/pod-product-compliance
Lightning Source LLC
Chambersburg PA
CBHW060120260626
47160CB00005B/1956